MEETING HIS MATCH

A MATCH ME STORY

KATEE ROBERT

Entangled Publishing, LLC
2614 South Timberline Road
Suite 109
Fort Collins, CO 80525
Visit our website at www.entangledpublishing.com.

Lovestruck is an imprint of Entangled Publishing, LLC.

Edited by Heather Howland and Kari Olson
Cover design by Heather Howland

Manufactured in the United States of America

First Edition July 2014

To Hawaii.
You're lucky that I don't know any matchmakers personally
or this book would be your life story.

Chapter One

Addison St. Claire hurried through the restaurant, hating that she was late. Punctuality wasn't usually a problem for her, but she'd been so busy arguing with one of her high-maintenance clients that she'd completely lost track of time.

If she could just convince Sarah Roberts to lower her standards a little, Addison was sure the woman would find happiness. But for Sarah, the perfect man seemed to equal dollar signs, so they'd been butting heads constantly over the choices in dates she'd made.

But that was neither here nor there. For the first time in what felt like months, she had a lunch appointment that was strictly pleasure and had nothing to do with interviewing potential clients of Connected at the Lips.

She nodded at the maître d' and moved deeper into the restaurant. The large windows overlooking the street let in plenty of sunlight, and the white and beige coloring only opened the small space up further. Even in a place filled with beautiful women and prominent New Yorkers, there was no mistaking Regan Wakefield. She was in a league all her own.

Regan smiled as she took the seat across the table. She looked as put-together as usual, her dark hair done up in an effortless professional style and her makeup without a single smudge. Happiness looked good on her. "Busy putting out fires?"

"As usual." Addison let out a pent-up breath she hadn't been aware she was holding. Of course Regan would understand her being late. The woman defined workaholic—or at least she had until she met her husband and had her twin girls. Speaking of… "How are things in paradise?"

"Oh, you know, the usual—the man is constantly rearranging our place just to screw with me, and he's nearly as busy as I am these days. And the girls are mobile. Every time I turn my back, Lizzie is climbing something and Jackie is finger-painting with her lunch." A dreamy look came into her dark eyes, one Addison recognized all too well. "But it's more than worth it, especially when Brock goes and does something sweet that sweeps me off my feet all over again. I never knew dads could be so damn sexy."

"Young love."

"Please. I'm three months younger than you." Regan leaned forward and studied her. "You've got circles the size of Utah under your eyes. What's up with that?"

Addison shifted and immediately held herself still. She'd known Regan would pick up on everything she didn't want to say. The woman was her very own Sherlock Holmes when it came to reading people. "Just working a lot."

"And not taking care of yourself." She smiled at the waitress as she took their drink order, and then turned that laser look back on Addison the moment the woman was gone. "You need a vacation."

"Probably." But who would she go with? Even if she were willing to leave her clients in the care of her team, the thought of traveling alone didn't do a single thing for her. If anything, it only compounded the loneliness that had seemed to get worse over time.

It used to be that helping other people find love was enough to fulfill her. Watching those first feelings evolve, listening to her clients tell her how excited they were about their dates with each other, helping them get to a point where they moved on without her assistance... It was enough to keep her warm at night.

Now it only seemed to remind her of what she'd lost.

Regan sipped her water. "I have the perfect solution."

She'd been pleasantly surprised when her friend called her up out of the blue. Now she wasn't so sure. "This isn't an intervention, is it?"

"Hardly." She laughed. "I happen to know a man in desperate need of a matchmaker, and you're the best there is."

Pleasure at the compliment wasn't nearly enough to banish her suspicion. "Why can't he call me himself?"

"Probably because he has no idea how in need he is."

She saw where this was going and shook her head. "I'm not going to ambush some poor guy because you've taken it into your head that he needs a wife."

"One, this so-called poor guy is my brother-in-law, so I'm entitled to meddle. Two, he's been dating—or failing to date—on his own for years now." She gave a wicked grin. "And, three, when have you ever known me to be wrong?"

That was the problem. Regan never was. Not when it

came to people. As a headhunter, she could get a good read on someone within two minutes of meeting them—usually less. That didn't mean Addison had to take the job, though. She nibbled on a breadstick, considering. What could a lunch hurt? She'd get a read on the man and decide if she wanted to take him on. After all Regan had done to help her out over the years, it was the least she could do. "I have a few free days next week. I could set up a consult."

"That's the thing. He's in Tennessee."

"*What*?" It was official. Her friend had gone round the bend. It was the only explanation for thinking Addison would do this.

"Look at it this way—you need a vacation. The South is nice this time of year and a hell of a lot warmer than New York. Just meet Caine. If it's a no-go, then you still have a few days to hang out and take in the *scenery*." The way she said the last word left nothing to the imagination. Regan seemed to take it almost personally that Addison hadn't been with anyone in years. She didn't understand that after having such a deep and amazing connection with Aiden, sex with anyone else was lukewarm at best.

And Addison *had* tried. It just wasn't in the cards for her.

But she knew a losing battle when she saw one. Plus, Regan was right—as usual. She couldn't remember the last time she'd slept through the night, and work just didn't hold the attraction it used to.

Maybe some time off would be exactly what she needed…

She took a drink of her water. "One meeting. If I don't like what I see or he's too difficult, then I'm off the hook."

Regan's smile sent a trickle of unease through her. "Oh, sweetie, I can almost guarantee you'll be taking this one on."

Chapter Two

Caine McNeill stared at the stack of paperwork on his desk and fought the urge to dump it in the trash. Or set it on fire. Nearly the entirety of McNeill Enterprises was digital these days, but his father refused to step into the twenty-first century. No, the old man still insisted on sending him the contracts for new clients on paper.

In triplicate.

For the twentieth time this week, he wondered what the fuck he was doing with his life. Yes, he'd nearly doubled the company's reach in the ten years he'd been CEO. He was one of the wealthiest men of his generation, and it couldn't all be laid at the feet of his trust fund.

But what had been challenging in his midtwenties was now old hat. McNeill Enterprises was in a totally stable place and, goddamn it, he was *bored*. Rationally, he knew it was time to move on to the next stage of his life. Get married, start a family, keep the business going for the next generation of McNeills.

Too bad dating took time—time he couldn't afford. His father had tried to balance family and work and had failed. Miserably. Caine wasn't too keen on bringing more people into his life just to neglect them.

But this was his life. Nothing was going change that, no matter how much he occasionally wanted it to. What would he do if he wasn't the CEO? He'd been groomed for this position since he was a kid. Even if he wanted to do something different, he didn't have a necessary skill set, and the opportunity to get one had passed.

As CEO, every problem landed on his shoulders, and it was a requirement of the job to hold up under the strain. It was how his old man did business, and the personal touch had made McNeill Enterprises the success it now was. The problem was this job didn't fulfill him the same way it seemed to fulfill his father.

He sighed. There was no help for it. Either he took care of the contracts now, or they'd be here waiting for him when he got in tomorrow morning. His phone rang, and pathetically glad for the distraction, he scrambled to answer. "McNeill."

"Mr. McNeill, there's an Addison St. Claire here to see you." Agnes, his secretary, sniffed. "She doesn't have an appointment and I already informed her that you are a *very* busy man." She lowered her voice. "She's been here nearly a half an hour and shows no signs of leaving."

He searched his memory, but the name rang no bells. It was tempting to tell Agnes to get rid of the woman, but the only thing he had on his plate in the immediate future was the damned paperwork. Recognizing that he was procrastinating, he said, "I can clear fifteen minutes."

Another sniff. "I'll send her in."

It was another fifteen minutes before the door opened, and Caine couldn't help his smile. Whatever this woman had said to his secretary, she must have really pissed her off. Agnes was usually the nicest lady in the world, but she could be a fire-breathing dragon when she felt her territory was being encroached on.

Then Addison St. Claire walked through his door and he forgot how to breathe.

It was *her*. The woman from his little brother Brock's wedding—the one he hadn't been able to take his eyes off through the entire reception. She wasn't flawless—not with her too-big brown eyes and pointed chin—but there had been a gracefulness to her movements that drew his attention six months ago. She'd been the one in charge of the twins—his new nieces—and she'd completely ignored him when he'd tried to catch her eye.

Granted, he hadn't tried *that* hard. It was his brother's wedding, after all, and he'd amused himself with watching Regan and his father circle each other. But throughout the entire thing, his gaze would inevitably find its way back to the redhead with the infectious smile that she seemed to aim only at the infants.

He sat behind his desk, staring like an idiot. Her clothing today wasn't outrageous, exactly, but it wasn't something he'd see walking down the streets of Manchester. The black dress hit all the right places, drawing attention to her body without flaunting it, but what got him were the black stockings. They hit about mid-thigh and, with the tall equally black heels, made her legs looks a mile long. They *should* have looked trashy, but the overall image she presented was professionally chic.

The sheer lust heating his body at the sight of her hit him like a ninety-mile-an-hour fastball to the head. He shot to his feet and then mentally cursed himself for looking so overeager. Why was she *here*?

She gave a perfectly polished smile. "Mr. McNeill? My name is Addison."

"I know." He winced at how abrupt that sounded and took her hand. "My secretary announced you." Her skin was soft against his palm, and he couldn't help but notice the bright teal tips of her fingernails.

"Of course." She frowned at their hands, and he realized that he'd held on entirely too long to be polite.

"Sorry." He jerked his hand back and tried to get his head on straight. This was ridiculous. He wasn't some bumbling teenager who'd seen a knockout for the first time in his life. He was the goddamn CEO of McNeill Enterprises.

It was time to act like it.

Caine sat back in his chair and watched her take a seat, trying not to notice the extra inch of skin revealed when she crossed her legs. She didn't seem flustered or nervous, so she'd obviously been in situations like this before. Whatever "this" was. He still had no idea why she was in his office. "What can I help you with, Ms. St. Claire?"

She sighed. "I take it you haven't talked to your sister-in-law lately?"

Alarm bells pealed through his head. He should have known. If she was at the wedding, it was because she was friends with the bride, and anything to do with the formidable Regan was enough to have him worried. She was a one-woman wrecking ball when it came to getting what she wanted. His father had sworn up and down and sideways that he'd never attend Brock's wedding to the New Yorker but, lo and behold, he'd been there for the ceremony and entire reception. He still hadn't been able to figure out what she'd done to make *that* happen.

But he wasn't about to show his unease to this stranger, no matter how captivating he'd found her. "Should I have?"

Another sigh. "I told her part of my conditions for coming down here was that she call you first." Addison shook her long mane of red hair. "I should have known she wouldn't give you any time to prepare."

The alarm bells in his head got louder. "What, exactly, should I be preparing for?"

"I'm New York's premier matchmaker. And apparently your sister-in-law thinks you need one. Desperately." She looked around his office. "I wasn't so sure when she put me up to this, but now I see her point."

Caine bristled. "I don't need a damn matchmaker."

"Are you sure? Just look at this place."

He followed the motion of her hand and saw nothing to draw the conclusion she so obviously had. The walls were painted a tasteful off-white and all the furniture was dark wood and hunter green. The paintings on the walls were landscapes—something he never would have chosen himself, but it set the professional tone an office should have. "I don't follow."

She leaned forward, all hesitance gone. If anything, her drive made her even more striking. "I have one question, and I need you to answer it honestly."

It sounded deceptively simple. He'd been around the

block enough times to know that meant it was anything but. "I'm listening."

"How many nights have you spent passed out there?" She pointed at the couch.

Shit. Guilt flared, even though he had nothing to feel guilty about. It shouldn't matter if he spent some nights—most nights—in his office. The couch was more than big enough to hold him, and he even had a personal shower and closet through the door Addison was now peering at.

Caine resisted the urge to cross his arms over his chest, but only barely. "Your point?"

"That you're CEO of one of the biggest companies south of the Mason-Dixon line and you still prefer to sleep in your office, rather than go home." She gave him a sympathetic look. "That obscenely large house gets awfully empty, doesn't it?"

So empty it echoed. It was yet another in a long line of battles he'd lost with his father. The McNeill family seat was meant to be filled to the brim with *family*, and it had been in generations past. Now, with Brock in New York and his parents in a flat in Nashville, it was only him to fill the massive space.

He hated it.

Addison didn't seem to need a response. She pursed her lips. "I really hadn't planned on doing more than meeting you, but Regan is right. If there ever was a man in need of a matchmaker, it's you."

"I do just fine for myself."

Again, a sympathetic look. As if she *pitied* him. "And how many women in the last five years have you been interested enough in to get into a serious relationship with?"

None, which she seemed to damn well know. The Addison who had looked so soft and sweet at a distance was apparently a mirage. *This* woman was just as formidable as his sister-in-law. He mentally cursed Regan and her meddling. "I don't know what she said to get you down here, but you're not needed."

"On the contrary, I'm desperately needed." She stood and smoothed down her dress, drawing his attention to the way her hips flared from her waist. That curve was deadly, the kind that seemed designed to fit a man's hands.

It was a crying shame the woman attached to it was such a goddamn nuisance. "Ms. St. Claire—"

"Regan already had my things sent to your house." She cast another glance at the couch. "I expect you to make it home tonight so we can get the questionnaire out of the way. This is obviously going to need a hands-on treatment."

Sadly, Caine had the sneaking suspicion that the kind of hands-on treatment he'd prefer from her had nothing to do with her intentions.

• • •

Addison didn't draw a full breath until she hit the sidewalk outside Caine's office. She should have known, having met the stunner that was Brock McNeill, that his older brother would be cut from the same cloth. If anything, he was even *more* attractive, as if that were even possible. Hell, it shouldn't have mattered—she'd dealt with plenty of attractive men in the past.

But none of them had shaken her like this one.

It wasn't the loneliness there on his face for anyone to

read who knew what to look for—loneliness was usually a driving factor that brought people to a matchmaker. She took that kind of thing at face value these days. It wasn't the nearly-OCD level of cleanliness of his office, either, that spoke of far too many hours behind that desk to be particularly healthy.

She pictured his face as she headed for the car she'd rented for her stay in Tennessee. Dark hair gone prematurely gray at the temples. Piercing gray eyes that must have come from his mother, because his father was colored darker, like Brock. A lean build that did nothing to hide the fact that he had to spend time in the gym. Even the close-cropped beard wasn't enough to truly throw her off her game, though it wasn't something she saw on CEOs...ever.

Now that she'd seen him again, she recognized him from the wedding. She'd caught him watching her once or twice, but she'd been so busy with Lizzie and Jackie that she hadn't put much thought behind it. Addison had made a mental note to ask Regan what his story was—Connected at the Lips could always use more attractive, successful men as clients—but she'd forgotten to pursue it when Lizzie spit up all over her dress.

She climbed into the car and turned it on, sighing at the feel of air-conditioning circulating in the front seat. Fall in New York had already begun, turning the air crisp and chilled. Apparently Tennessee hadn't gotten the memo, because it was a humid seventy-five degrees. That must be her problem, because she certainly wasn't flustered from the heated look Caine had sent her as she walked into the office.

Even worse was the answering heat that had flared low in her body.

It caught her so off guard, she'd almost tripped over her own feet. Needing a distraction, she dialed her phone and pulled onto the street. It barely rang once.

"You're there already?"

The fact that Regan was obviously sitting on her phone, waiting for this call, only reaffirmed what she'd already known. "You didn't tell him I was coming."

"Nope." She didn't even have the decency to sound sorry. "Will you take him on?"

"He doesn't want me to." In fact, he'd seemed adamant that he was doing just fine on his own, poor misguided soul that he was. She wasn't in the habit of forcing her services on unwilling people, but she'd also never met a person who needed her more than Caine McNeill did—whether he knew it or not. He wasn't happy, and probably hadn't been for quite some time. She knew all too well about that kind of insidious misery, the one that never seemed to go away no matter what a person did.

"That's not an answer."

Still, she hesitated. The only reason she was down here in the first place was because even after years, she still hadn't figured out a way to successfully say no to Regan. "It's going to be impossible to get him on a date if he's not willing."

"That's what drugs are for. I think a little pot brownie could loosen him right up."

"Regan!"

"Oh, fine, I was kidding. Mostly. Just use that St. Claire charm you're so famous for. He won't stand a chance."

She wasn't so sure. But for the first time in nearly a year, adrenaline coursed through Addison's system and good vibes bubbled up inside her. It had been so long since the thought of a match made her feel alive that she almost didn't know what to do with it. But if there was one thing Caine McNeill needed, it was his soul mate. The fact that he didn't seem to know that only made the challenge of finding her more difficult. "He'll be a tough sell."

"The toughest. These McNeill men are crazy stubborn." Regan laughed. "Give it a day and see what you can pull off. I have faith."

Of course she did. She was safe in New York with the love of her life, not trying to bully a millionaire into letting her match him with a stranger. Addison tapped her finger on her steering wheel. Damn it, she knew better. Her friend wouldn't shy away from a challenge like this. No, Regan would *relish* it—kind of like she was in danger of doing right now.

Maybe she was right—again—and this was exactly what Addison needed, even more so than a vacation. "I'll see what I can do."

"You got the key to the house I sent?"

"I'm on my way out there now." She'd stopped by a hotel for a few hours after her plane landed to freshen up and get her game face on, so she hadn't had a chance to check out this house she'd read about. Apparently it had been in the McNeill family since before the Civil War—unsurprisingly, they'd fought for the Confederacy—and had nearly as many legends surrounding it as the family itself did. There were a ton of ghost stories, though she couldn't imagine George McNeill letting ghost hunters desecrate his family seat.

"Perfect. Keep me updated, and don't forget to have fun while you're down there. Be sure to check out the piano room—I bet you haven't played in forever." Then she was gone, leaving Addison to follow the GPS directions out of Manchester.

As she drove, she mentally compiled a list of things she'd need before she actually picked the potential matches for Caine. He had to fill out the questionnaire, if only to give her a good idea of what he thought he wanted. Addison had learned a long time ago that what people put on paper wasn't necessarily what they needed, but she liked to have a baseline to judge by.

After that... She shook her head. Regan hadn't been joking when she said Caine required work. He might be rich and attractive, but there was something beneath the surface that she couldn't quite put her finger on yet. It didn't fit with the image of the millionaire CEO or with the list of truly impressive achievements she'd found when she did a cursory background search on him. The man the public saw was the perfect oldest son of George McNeill, who seemed more than happy to follow in his father's footsteps.

The thing was, even if Regan hadn't dangled the knowledge in front of her when she offered this job, Addison would have known the truth the second she laid eyes on him.

Caine McNeill was miserable.

Chapter Three

Caine opened his eyes and immediately closed them again, hoping like hell that he was dreaming. But when he tried again, he got the same result. Addison St. Claire was in his office. Again. And she didn't look happy. He sighed and sat up, knocking over the pile of contracts he'd been working on when he must have passed out. "How'd you get past Agnes?"

"Trade secret." She surveyed him with a critical eye, and he had the feeling he came up short. "Maybe I didn't make myself clear yesterday. For this to work, I'll need your cooperation—which means no more nights spent on that couch."

He scrubbed a hand over his face. "That's the funny thing—I didn't ask for this. I'd be perfectly happy to get you a car to the airport and send you back to wherever you came from."

"Would you?" She leaned forward, drawing his attention

to the fact that she was wearing purple today. The dress wasn't particularly low-cut, but there was no hiding *those* curves. She cleared her throat and he realized he'd been staring at her breasts. Addison raised an eyebrow, but continued as if she hadn't just caught him ogling her. "Can you honestly tell me that you're living a happy and fulfilled life?" When he opened his mouth, she said, "*Honestly.*"

Though it was tempting to lie just to get her out of here, he couldn't do it with those brown eyes pinning him in place. "I do well enough."

"I'll be sure to tell your brother to put that on your gravestone. Caine McNeill—he did well enough."

Christ, what a depressing thought. But he wasn't about to bare his soul to this woman who thought she had his number. She didn't need to know that he enjoyed the work he did, but he didn't love it. He never had. He'd gone through life meeting every challenge his father expected, and he was proud of what he'd accomplished. But there had never been another option for him. He wasn't sure what he would have picked for himself if there *were* other options.

It wasn't something he liked thinking about.

Annoyed that he *was* thinking about it because of her, he glared. "Why are you so concerned with my happiness?"

"Because everyone deserves to find their soul mate."

He laughed. "Soul mate. That's rich. Aren't you a little old to be believing in fairy tales?"

"Laugh all you want. I have an excellent track record of successful matches and, as I said last night, you're desperately in need of a successful match. Which brings us to what you *should* have accomplished last night." She held up a stack of papers stapled together. "We need to go through this questionnaire before I can be effective."

"That's a damn shame, because I don't have time. I have this little company I'm in charge of running." He pushed to his feet, hoping like hell that Agnes had a chance to get his dirty clothes from last week to the dry cleaners and back. If not, he was going to have to actually leave the office or run the risk of looking like he'd slept here overnight.

Coffee wouldn't be a terrible idea, either.

He turned, effectively dismissing her, and headed into the bathroom off the back of his office. She was a smart enough woman. Hopefully she'd be gone by the time he completely woke up. Caine splashed water on his face and brushed his teeth, and he couldn't help listening for the sound of the door to his office closing. Addison might be beautiful and set on matching him, but even she could take a hint. He wasn't interested.

But when he opened the door, she was still perched on the end of the chair where she'd been sitting when he woke up. He sighed. "You're making it difficult to be polite."

"I'm not the only one." Her smile didn't so much as flicker. "The faster we get this done, the faster I can get out of your hair."

Persistent, wasn't she? But if she was friends with Regan, that made sense. "Don't make me threaten to call security."

"Good Lord." She got to her feet and strode around the couch until she was in his face. "What are you so afraid of? That I might be right?"

This close, he caught a whiff of her perfume, something light and airy that made him think of the ocean. It was almost enough to distract him from the urge to pick her up and dump her ass outside his office door. Almost. "I'm not afraid of a damn thing except a nuisance of a woman who won't take a goddamn hint."

Her smile widened, as if he'd just confirmed something. "Perfect. Then there's no reason *not* to let me have a crack at it."

What part of what he'd just said made her think he'd actually entertain this crazy idea? Caine stepped forward, crowding her. It was a bully move and he wasn't proud of it, but he'd left his common sense behind when he woke up to her invading his space. "There's every reason."

She lifted her chin. "Name one."

"How about the fact I can't look at you in that dress without wanting to find out what's beneath it?"

She blinked, her perfectly lipsticked pink mouth going into a surprised O. Hell, she wasn't the only one surprised. He hadn't meant to say that out loud, but there was something about this woman that rubbed him in all sorts of uncomfortable ways. She'd been in his presence less than fifteen minutes and she was already bringing things to the forefront that he'd spent a lifetime fighting to control.

And he couldn't stop if he wanted to.

"Why do you look so shocked?" He moved closer, until they were nearly chest to chest. "You're a beautiful woman, even if you're aggravating the hell out of me right now."

She seemed to fight to regain control of her expression. "You're insane."

He sure as hell felt it right now. He fought against the desire to touch her. Pushing her with proximity was one thing, but hooking the back of her neck and hauling her in for a kiss was crossing a serious line. He wasn't a goddamn savage.

No matter how much he felt like one right now.

She glared, but he didn't miss the way her body leaned into his, like a flower seeking the sun. If he kissed her right now, would she kiss him back or punch him in the face? The fact that he didn't know only intrigued him further, which meant he had to get her the hell out of here before he did something truly stupid. "Just another reason why you should get your ass on a plane home. Today."

• • •

Addison couldn't make herself move back, no matter how loud the voice inside her became demanding she do just that. Annoyance had to be the reason she was staring at his mouth and wondering what it would be like to kiss him. The *only* reason. She hadn't had a challenge in so long that the thrill of being faced with one was enough to make her as crazy as he apparently was. He was so much bigger this close, his height dwarfing her even in her heels, and his shoulders making him loom.

That's when she realized exactly what he was doing.

She jerked back, taking a few extra steps to put the nearest chair between them. When he merely watched her with an impassive expression on his face, her suspicion was confirmed. "You're trying to intimidate me into leaving."

"Did it work?"

Almost. The door was far too tempting when she was still having a hard time keeping her gaze on his eyes instead of that wicked curve of his bottom lip. If she left now, she wouldn't have to face the fact that a part of her she thought long dead perked up just by being in his presence. It didn't matter what she felt physically, though. Caine was destined for another woman.

A good thing, too, because he was obviously a handful.

Addison had dealt with clients who were a handful before. She could do it again. She very pointedly ignored the fact that none of her clients in the past had affected her on this same level, and focused back on Caine. He hadn't moved, but the room felt smaller with him staring at her so intently. She shoved her hair back. "Stop it."

"I'm not doing anything."

Yes, he was. She took a deep breath that did nothing to make her feel less hunted. Damn it, she was better than this. "You're trying to make me uncomfortable, but it won't work." That was a dirty lie, though she was more uncomfortable by the way her body was reacting than anything else. "I think you'll find I don't scare easily."

"You know, I've changed my mind."

She froze, sensing a trap and unable to figure out where it was. "You...have."

"I reckon maybe you're right. Maybe I do need a woman—"

"Soul mate." If he could settle for just any woman, Regan wouldn't have needed to call her in. "The only way it'll be a successful match is if it's with your soul mate."

"Whatever you choose to call it." He dropped onto the couch and patted the cushion next to him. "Show me this questionnaire."

There was definitely something up. A man like Caine was far too stubborn to go from ready to call security to agreeing with her. It didn't matter that she *was* right. The fact he'd done a one-eighty with no warning had her suspicious.

But she wasn't going to turn down a chance to get this

ball rolling. The sooner she got him matched up, the sooner she could go back to New York and get away from this strange fluttering in her stomach. Addison scooped up the papers and took a seat on the other side of the couch, leaving two whole cushions between them. She turned to the first page of the questionnaire, trying not to think about the fact that Caine had slept on this very couch last night, or that he looked deliciously rumpled right now, his tie askew and his shirt wrinkled. He looked almost approachable.

At least, he would if she were into the overbearing alpha male type thing.

She gave herself a mental shake. It didn't matter what she might or might not be into. Right now was about finding out what *he* was into so she could start narrowing down possible candidates. She cleared her throat. "First question—"

"You can't expect me to be able to read that from all the way over here." Before she could bring up the fact that she didn't actually expect that since she was reading him the damn questions, he moved closer. A whole lot closer. With bare inches between them—less than that when he stretched his arm over the back of the couch—the only way they could be closer was if she were in his lap. The fact that he *still* hadn't touched her only ramped up her awareness of how little distance there was between them.

Caine grinned. "That's better."

Not by a long shot. Maybe she should have done this portion over the phone, because at this rate, she'd be lucky if she didn't fling herself away from him just to escape the horrible longing to touch him. Or, worse, give in and actually touch him.

She braced herself. She could get through these questions

and then she'd have plenty of space to get her head on straight. "What do you look for in a partner?"

"Going for gold right off the bat, huh?" He leaned over to peer at the paper, putting his face nearly against hers.

Good grief. She batted him away. "Stop trying to crowd me and answer the question."

"Fine. I reckon if and when I end up getting married, I need a woman who's independent enough to handle the fact that I work long hours. She needs to have her own thing going on because I won't be able to entertain her. I'm expected to have a family, too."

Grateful for a reason to focus on anything other than how good he smelled—something woodsy and masculine— she grabbed a pen off the table and started taking notes. The way he spoke wasn't exactly enthusiastic, but she could work with it. She paused when he didn't continue. "What else?"

"That's all."

The fact that he didn't realize the problem put her back on firmer ground. "Those are pretty basic things—she has a life outside you and she wants children. If that's all you wanted, you'd be married by now." When he just stared at her, she prompted, "What about hobbies? Interests? Stuff that you like outside of work that you'd want to share with a significant other?"

"I don't get much free time."

She waited, but he didn't seem all that inclined to help her out. "There has to be something you do besides work." Even as she said it, she wondered if maybe there *wasn't.* God, this man really was on the road to needing a full-scale intervention.

"There isn't."

That just wouldn't do. "Then we'll find you something." She made a note to dig deeper and see what kind of extra-curricular activities he'd been involved in during his school years. Maybe the answer was there. "You have to have something besides work to talk about on the dates I'll set you up on. That's the surest way to ensure you don't get a second one."

"And here I thought I'd get by on my charm and good looks."

"That'll get you a first date. It won't get you a second one with anyone who'd be suitable." When he laughed, she looked up from her notes. Holy hell, the man had laugh lines to rival his little brother's. Then what he'd said hit her. "My God, did you just make a joke?"

"It's been known to happen."

If forbidding Caine had been attractive, a laughing Caine was downright deadly. What was she supposed to do with a man who was unhappy and driven and had a sly sense of humor? Flustered, she turned back to her notes. *Keep to the questions and get out of here.* "What about physical aspects? Is there anything you refuse to compromise on? A certain type you gravitate toward?" She usually encouraged clients to let go of their "types" and focus on the person beneath the physical, but she liked to know what they liked.

"I seem to have developed a keen fascination with redheads."

She shot him a look. "You're doing it again." She just wished it didn't send heat coursing through her body. He was trying to manipulate her into letting him have his way. It didn't mean anything.

Sadly, her hormones weren't listening.

"I don't have a physical preference. Beautiful, I reckon. She's got to be able to doll herself up and attend the functions where my presence is required."

Addison had had plenty of clients who gave her so much information she basically had to mine out the truth to discover what they actually wanted. Caine was the exact opposite. "So, let me get this straight. You have no hobbies. You don't care what this woman looks like as long as she can 'doll herself up' and entertain herself and pop out a few babies for you?"

His gray eyes gave away nothing, but she again had the sneaking suspicion that he was testing her. "That sounds about right."

He might as well not have agreed to anything, because he was setting her up to fail.

Addison smiled because she felt like smacking that smug look right off his face. "I'll see what I can do." Because she had her work cut out for her. Even if she could find a woman he was interested in, getting that candidate to like *him* was going to be challenging. He might be a millionaire, but most women wanted a man a few personality traits beyond being ambitious and rude. She'd have to work on that before she picked who she'd fly down here to test the waters.

But it was nothing she could do right this second. First she needed more research, and then she needed to form a plan of action. Maybe Regan would have some ideas about that. She stood and smoothed down her dress, painfully aware of the way Caine's gaze tracked the movement. "I'll let you get to work. We'll talk more when you come home tonight." Because he *would* come back to the giant house she'd stayed in last night, or she'd drive over here and

pester him until he left. She didn't know how he stood living there alone, but one night of it and she was jumping at
small sounds, flinching at shadows, and ready to believe in
all those ghost stories she wished she hadn't read before she
flew down here. No wonder the man was so cranky.

He smiled in a way that did nothing good for her blood
pressure. "I wouldn't miss it for the world."

Chapter Four

The day went downhill after Addison left. As fun as poking at her had been, he couldn't deny there was a spark of something there. If she hadn't pulled away when she did, he would have said to hell with personal boundaries and kissed her. Caine spent entirely too much of his morning wondering what she would taste like. Would she be sweet like she'd seemed at Brock's wedding? Or tart like her personality now canted toward? Not knowing drove him nuts.

He had to put the conundrum out of his head, though, when his father called. He took a deep breath and answered. "Father."

"Have you got those contracts finished yet?"

Even after all these years, he couldn't help the disappointment that hit him. There wouldn't be any small talk today, just like there hadn't been any for the last thirty-odd years. His old man wasn't interested in what he was doing with his life as long as he was managing the company and meeting the other expectations laid out for him. It was a lack he'd always felt, though he'd done his damnedest never to show it. "I'll have them back to you shortly."

"You should have had them back to me last night."

The thing his younger brother never understood was that Caine didn't live up to their father's high expectations any more than Brock did. The only difference between them was that he never stopped trying. There were days when he envied his brother's ability to tell their old man to fuck off. He'd never quite managed it. "I'm sorry."

"Don't be sorry. Get it done faster next time." A voice murmured in the background. "My nine o'clock's here. I expect those papers on my desk in an hour."

Since it took an hour to get from Manchester to Nashville, he'd have to send them out the door right now. Fighting back a sigh, he said, "Will do." Caine hung up, the good mood that had come from needling Addison disappearing like smoke. As well it should. He didn't have time to play games with her, no matter how delightful her responses to his pushing were. When he got home tonight, he'd set the record straight and send her on her way.

Satisfied he had the situation well in hand, he settled down to finish the contracts. Once he gave them to Agnes to be sent over, he moved on. There was a new development going in north of Manchester, and he fully intended on securing the vast stretch of property just north of it—if he could get Gloucester and Richards to see eye to eye. Right now it was a field, but inside of ten years, it would be the premier place for small businesses and for people from the new suburbs who didn't want to drive the fifteen minutes back into town. It was a good long-term investment all the way around.

By the time he surfaced, his stomach rumbling a pro-test, it was after five. Caine scrubbed a hand over his face. As tempting as it was to order in and keep going, he had a matchmaker to deal with. He allowed himself a smile as he thought of how outraged she looked when she was going through that questionnaire. He'd answered honestly enough, but seeing how baffled she was had made him be purpose-fully vague going forward.

He shut off his computer and grabbed his keys. It wouldn't hurt to go home for once. At least the house wouldn't be empty—Caine had a feeling that any house Addison was in could never be termed as such. She was too full of life, and that enthusiasm leached out into the room around her.

Even if she was a pain in his ass.

Agnes was already gone for the day, but she'd left a new pot of coffee going for him. He shook his head. She was an amazing secretary, but it said something sad about his life that she automatically assumed he'd be working late. It wasn't the predictability that bothered him so much as the fact he had nowhere else to go.

This was his life.

Caine headed for home, the drive doing nothing to re-lax him, mostly because he knew exactly what was waiting for him at the house. Or, rather, *who*. God only knew what trouble Addison had gotten up to today. He should be re-lieved she hadn't dropped by the office again or insisted on staying to talk more about this matchmaking nonsense, but he couldn't stop thinking about the way she'd leaned into him when he'd gotten within touching distance. Which led him to wonder when was the last time she'd been that close to another person, let alone a man.

A long time ago, if the surprise on her face was any indication.

He pulled into his long, winding driveway, cursing his curiosity. It didn't matter that the matchmaker was engaging and stirred something inside him that he thought long gone. She was a complication he didn't need.

But knowing that didn't make him any less reluctant to send her on her way. She was a breath of fresh air that he hadn't realized he'd needed, even if it'd come when they were verbally sparring and poking at each other.

Caine opened his front door and froze as a vicious growl echoed through the foyer. What the fuck? Before he could pinpoint its source, Addison came flying around the corner. "Gollum, *no*. He's a friend!" She pointed a finger and he followed her gaze to a giant white mop standing in the shadow of the stairs, its lip peeled back to reveal a truly impressive set of teeth. The idiot woman didn't seem the least bit intimidated. "Be nice. He's not going to hurt your pups."

Pups?

The dog ducked its head and rubbed against the side of Addison's leg, still staring warily at Caine. She finally turned her attention to him and smiled. "Welcome home."

This place hadn't felt like home in a very long time. The fact he now had someone here waiting for him—even temporarily—felt strange. He pushed that away to focus on the immediate problem. "What the hell is that monstrosity?"

"Shh." She put her hands over the dog's ears. "Don't call her that. You'll hurt her feelings."

God forbid. "Fine. What is that massive dog that I don't

remember owning doing here?" He hoped like hell he had misheard her when she said pups, because one giant mop of a dog was more than enough to deal with right now.

"She's here to help." When he just stared, she smiled harder. "We talked about this."

"No, we didn't. I would remember agreeing to get a dog."

"You're letting me work on your image. Gollum will improve it."

He eyed the animal. "Tolkien's Gollum was male."

"Well, this Gollum is female." She patted the dog's head. "She's quite nice once she gets used to you."

He doubted it. The animal looked more likely to take his hand off at the wrist than cuddle up with him. So much for dogs being man's best friend. "That's wonderful to hear, but I never agreed to any of this."

Addison sighed. "I won't be able to successfully match you if you don't work with me, Caine."

The fact that he hadn't volunteered for this matchmaking business seemed lost on her. He stepped forward, but stopped when the dog growled again. "What does successfully matching me have to do with a damn dog?"

"Gollum will make you more approachable. You need that—desperately."

"There's not a damn thing approachable about that beast."

"Something you have in common."

He circled them, eyeing the long dreads hanging from the dog. It really did look like a mop. When he was a kid, he'd desperately wanted a dog. His dad had refused to allow it. As much as it had broken his ten-year-old heart, he wasn't about to make up for the lack now.

Besides, if he'd picked a dog, it certainly wouldn't be this one. "It—" He corrected himself when she glared. "*She* looks like a mop."

"And this is exactly the problem." She waved at his entire body. "You can't even stop yourself from insulting an innocent animal. How am I supposed to get you ready for decent company?"

"I've been passing in decent company for years." No matter how much he hated playing the political games being CEO demanded of him.

But Addison apparently wasn't listening. "For your information, Gollum is a komondor. They're a breed with bold and majestic history."

"A history of cleaning floors?"

She hissed like an angry cat. "In World War II, when the Nazis invaded Hungary, these dogs wouldn't stop defending their families until they were killed. As long as they were alive, they wouldn't stop, wouldn't compromise, wouldn't give in. Sound familiar?"

From the way she was looking at him, she obviously thought those were traits he and the beast shared. "I reckon I've made quite the impression on you for you to have such a high opinion of me."

Her eyes flashed. "Something like that."

Before he could respond, movement in the doorway behind her caught his eye. Four white fluff balls tumbled into the room, yipping as they ran in circles around Gollum and Addison. Jesus Christ.

Caine gritted his teeth. "Tell me those aren't *puppies*."

For the first time since he walked through the door, she looked less than a hundred percent sure of herself. "They're only eight weeks old. I couldn't take her babies away from her." She brightened. "Plus, this just shows how big of a heart you have."

She certainly had a lot of ideas about his supposed image if she thought he needed a herd of dogs to be more approachable. "Except it wasn't my idea."

"Semantics."

The dog stopped eyeing him long enough to follow her pups into another room. It was the strangest thing. Caine could actually *see* his life spiraling out of control. "I'm billing you for any damage to my carpets and furniture."

"No need to be so sour about it. Komondors actually shed less than your average dog."

And this was why he didn't have a dog. Things like shedding and potty training and coming home at regular hours to make sure the animal was fed. "I don't have time for a dog."

"Then you don't have time for a wife. A dog is significantly less of a commitment."

"If you'd be so polite as to remember...I *don't* want a wife." Or at least he didn't have time for a wife. Running the company meant long nights and taking his work home with him...when he actually managed to make it home. Call him crazy, but the thought of entering into a marriage like his parents had—cold and functioning independent of each other—wasn't appealing in the least.

"Maybe not, but you certainly need one." She peered out into the driveway where he'd parked and groaned. "A convertible Jaguar? In red? Seriously? Don't you have something...subtler?"

Now she was picking at his car? Christ. He'd only been home fifteen minutes and all she'd done so far was insult him. "Subtler."

"Something that doesn't scream 'I have money and am a powerful man!' would be good."

"Plenty of women like my car."

She shot him a look that was damn near pitying. *Again.* "And how well has that worked out?"

Damn it. There wasn't a damn thing he could do to argue with that one particular fact.

Needing to be back on firmer ground, he stepped closer to her. Her breath caught when he tucked a long strand of hair behind her ear, and a thread of satisfaction worked through him. She wanted him. She might not like that she wanted him, but she did. "You tell me."

"Stop trying to change the subject or intimidate me into retreating. I'm going through candidates tonight. It might be difficult, but I'm sure I can find someone suitable." She surveyed him again, taking a few steps back. "I suppose your wardrobe is adequate."

He was wearing a thousand-dollar suit and she found that *adequate*? Every word that came out of her mouth was a surprise, and damn if that didn't send a thrill through him. Ever since he was a child, he knew the path his life would take. The last thirty-odd years, he'd walked it in exactly the right way—one that didn't involve surprises. And Addison was nothing but surprises. But that didn't mean he'd let her get away with the last word. "I see you're still wearing the purple dress."

She blushed, smoothing down the dress in a nervous movement that only served to accent her body. And what a body it was. She looked soft and inviting and curvy in all the right places. Combined with the brilliant red hair—and the personality to match—it was enough to make his mouth water. He stalked closer, edging her up against the wall. "I like you in purple."

"I didn't pick it for you." She stopped him with a hand on his chest, but she didn't remove it, her fingers kneading his pec. He didn't think she realized she was doing it, because she was too busy frowning at him. "Stop trying to intimidate me. It won't work."

"Addison, did it ever occur to you that I'm not the kind of man who tries to physically intimidate women into submission?"

She raised an eyebrow. "Recent experience seems to contradict that, don't you think?"

Damn it, she had a point. Ever since she waltzed into his office, he'd been crowding her without invitation and generally acting like a shit. Caine started to step back, but her grip on his shirt tightened, keeping him in place. He went still, as fascinated by the confused look on her face as by the warmth of her touch against his chest. She stared at her hand like it didn't belong to her. "Um…"

If he were a better man, he'd extract himself from this situation and let her retreat. He wasn't a better man. He closed the small distance between them and did what he'd wanted to do ever since he set eyes on her.

He cupped the back of her neck and kissed her.

Chapter Five

Addison's world caught fire at the feel of Caine's lips against hers. It burned through everything she thought she knew, through her expectations, and finally, through her body itself. All in the space between one heartbeat and the next. Every cell of her being wanted to throw herself at him and hang on until the fire raged out. Because it had to rage out eventually. An attraction that flared this strongly off a single kiss couldn't possibly last for more than an instant.

But what if it didn't?

That question had her shoving him away so hard that her back hit the wall. He barely moved, just stood there, ruining her life with the desire written over his face. "Addison—"

She couldn't catch her breath. She couldn't think. Letting her client—even a reluctant client—kiss her was breaking her rules. Wanting to do it again? Unforgivable. "You've got to stop doing this."

"Doing what? This is the first time I've kissed you."

"You know what I mean. Stop trying to bully me."

"Do you really want me to?"

Yes, she did. Hadn't she just said that? But she couldn't quite make herself let go of his shirt. In fact, she found herself pulling him closer, inch by inch, as if drawn by a gravitational pull she couldn't resist. He'd undone the top few buttons at some point during the day and that slice of skin at the top of his chest called to her.

Maybe Regan was onto something with her theory about pent-up sexual frustration, because Addison suddenly couldn't think of a single reason why she shouldn't kiss Caine again.

So she did.

She went up onto her tiptoes and pressed her lips to his. It was nearly as innocent as what he'd just done to her, but it didn't stay that way. The fire that had banked when she pushed him away flared back up with a vengeance. She parted her lips, and he took full advantage, stroking her tongue with his, exploring her mouth as if he had every right. And Addison could only cling to him and return the favor.

He backed her against the wall, pinning her there with the weight of his body, keeping one hand on her hip and the other buried in her hair. It felt good, but she needed more. She needed *touch*. Skin on skin. The slide of his body against her own. She needed it so much, she could barely breathe.

Caine kissed along her jaw and down her throat, but stopped just short of the strap of her dress. She wanted to tell him to keep going, to not stop until she was lost. Damn it, *no*. This was wrong. She'd had her chance at love and it had ended all too soon. She wasn't going to ruin Caine's just because he made her feel good.

Soul mates only came around once in a lifetime.

"Stop."

He immediately backed off. Her knees tried to buckle, but she leaned against the wall and managed to avoid falling. Any hope that he missed the move died at the grin on his face. "You taste better than I'd guessed."

Don't blush, don't you dare... Crap. She looked away. "Now that you've satisfied your curiosity, we can move on." A little part of her died at the thought of never having his hands on her again, but she silenced it. She wasn't here to kiss Caine—or do anything else with him. She was here to help him find his soul mate. End of story.

"Oh, darlin', I don't think so."

She jerked around so fast, she cricked her neck. "What?"

His smile widened. "All you've done is whetted my curiosity. It would take a whole lot more to satisfy it."

Unbidden images thrust themselves to the forefront of her mind of just what that might entail. Sex. Definitely sex. She let herself consider it for half a second—of having a fling with him until she found him the right woman—and then made herself discard it. If one kiss could have her thinking about compromising her hard-and-fast rules, sex would throw them out the window completely.

That wasn't an option. "No."

"No?"

"That's what I said. This was a mistake. It's not happening again." Maybe if she said that enough times, she'd actually start to believe it.

From the look on his face, he didn't believe it any more than she did. "I'll make you a deal."

"I'm listening." Just like before, his doing a one-eighty only meant trouble for her. She was sure of it. For someone with a relatively clean reputation business-wise, this man sure was sneaky.

"I won't kiss you again." Before she could breathe a sigh of relief, he continued, "But next time you kiss me, all bets are off."

Addison's jaw dropped. "I'm not kissing you again." Her entire body perked up at the thought, but she told it to shut the hell up.

"I guess we'll see, won't we?" He picked up the briefcase he'd set on the floor while she'd introduced him to Gollum. "Have a good night, darlin'. I trust you'll be sleeping just as well as I will."

Only if he meant he wouldn't sleep a wink. She refused to show just how much his calm determination threw her, though. "Like a baby."

"Whatever you have to tell yourself." He turned and walked up the staircase, and damn her self-control, she checked out his ass the entire time. It was only after he disappeared down the hallway at the top of the stairs that she managed to move.

God, she was in so much trouble.

Needing to put as much space between them as possible—and there was a hell of a lot of it in this place to put between them—she made her way to where she'd set up beds for Gollum and her pups. It was on the far side of the house, right next to the door to both the greenhouse and the rest of the grounds. She let the dogs out, pausing to pat Gollum on the head, and then settled down on the fainting couch with her computer.

Obviously she couldn't be trusted to spend more time with Caine than strictly necessary, so she had to get a move on with finding him his match. Easier said than done. It was more than his questionable answers about what he wanted — there was the distance factor as well. Ninety percent of Connected at the Lips' clients were in the New York tristate area, which was a hell of a long way from Tennessee.

So the first thing she had to do was narrow the field down to women who would be willing to move. Caine wasn't going anywhere, so she refused to waste time with something that would turn into a long-distance relationship permanently. But she had a decent number of candidates who could — and would — move.

The trick was making Caine an attractive enough catch to get them down here in the first place.

Her face heated. He definitely had his high points, but she couldn't exactly list his kissing skills as an asset. And as she'd told him, the money wasn't enough, either. There were plenty of men with money in the city. His appearance was a good start, and the man could dress. Her fingers twitched, it being all too easy to recall how good his shirt felt beneath her hands.

And, Lord, was he driven when he put his mind to something. Having all that attention focused on her was enough to make her wonder what he'd be like in a relationship…

"Get a grip and focus." She took a deep breath and got to work. She had her list narrowed down to eight women when the dog scratched at the door to be let back in. Addison smiled at the trail of puppies behind her. She hadn't meant to end up with a herd of animals, but the thought of separating a mother from her babies had hit her in the chest. They were nearly weaned, but they'd cried when the guy took Gollum out of the cage. She couldn't leave them behind.

Caine wasn't too happy about them being here, but he would just have to deal with it. A mother shouldn't have to be separated from her babies.

She recognized her vehemence on the subject as a little bit irrational, but it was too late to worry about it now. He needed things in his life to make him more approachable, and Gollum fit the bill.

Now, if she could only fix his sexual underhandedness and stubborn streak as easily.

• • •

"That woman is on the phone again."

Caine rubbed the bridge of his nose. Ever since Addison had sneaked into his office, Agnes refused to call her by name. With yet another stack of contracts on his desk and an angry developer on his back, he didn't have time for this. If one element of the Richards deal fell through, the entire thing would turn into a shitstorm. "Put her through."

"Who does she think she is? You don't have time for her to be calling every three seconds. She's a disrespectful little—"

"Agnes." He'd known she didn't like the woman, but this was beyond what he'd expected. Which meant he had to smooth Agnes's feathers or she'd be mother-henning him for the rest of the day. Goddamn it. "I'm sorry you don't like her, but she's a business associate." Who was making his life a hell of a lot harder than it had to be.

"She's interfering with your day and you're a very busy man, Mr. McNeill."

And this conversation wasn't helping. He bit back a sigh. "Please put her through."

"Yes, sir."

The line clicked. "Addison—"

"I only have fifteen minutes and your receptionist took up twelve of them."

When had his life come down to women battling over his time? If someone had told him this would happen five years ago, he'd have laughed and patted himself on the back for being a lothario for once in his life. In reality, they pulled him out of his office only long enough to suit their needs — and argue over him like dogs with a bone — and then they kicked him back out again. It wasn't the high point of his life, that was for damn sure. "You know, I have a job that requires my attention."

"I'm aware. But unless you want to spend the rest of your life sleeping on that couch, this also requires your attention."

It had been two days since their kiss, and she'd successfully retreated behind a professional mask. He didn't like it one bit. But he'd told her he wouldn't touch her again until she kissed him, so he wouldn't. But that didn't mean he couldn't push her a little in the meantime. "I have something else that requires your attention."

"That's cute, but no, thank you." And then she carried on without missing a beat. "I'm arranging for a woman to fly in next week, so I need you to put her on your schedule."

Holy shit, this was actually happening. He'd gone along with the matchmaking questions, mostly so he could spend more time with Addison, but actually having to go on dates was another thing altogether. "I don't think—"

"That was not a request, Caine. I've already booked the flight. If you don't meet her, she'll have come down here for nothing and it will be a black mark on my reputation as a matchmaker. I might even lose her as a client."

Christ. He wanted to tell her that he didn't give a damn…

but it would be a lie. What could a few dates hurt? "Fine."

"I'll email you the day and time, though I'd appreciate if you suggested a restaurant since I'm not familiar with the area. Something expensive but understated."

"Jean Claude's."

"I'll take care of the reservations."

He didn't like this painfully cold woman on the other end of the line. If she kept up this matchmaking business, eventually she was going to... He paused. Going to what? Leave and head back to New York? What else would she do? He might be attracted to her, but that didn't mean he wanted her as a permanent fixture in his life. Caine cleared his throat. "Do I get a chance to look at this woman and the ones that come after her? Or do I not have a say?"

"If you remember correctly—and you should since it was two days ago—you told me you don't have any preferences beyond her being beautiful. I can assure you that anyone I bring down here will be beautiful."

He shoved any thoughts of Addison out of his head. The least he could do was actually go on the dates. It didn't mean that he was going to marry whomever she paraded in front of him, and *not* cooperating meant she would eventually get fed up and leave. He wasn't ready to see her walk out of his life just yet. "I'll make sure to clear my calendar."

"Good."

"Good." He hung up, hating the feeling in his chest. It was like a toothache, but there was no definitive source. It didn't matter. He had too much work to do to worry about whatever Addison was getting up to in his house without him.

Or how empty it would be when she finished her mission and left.

Chapter Six

Addison set the phone down and tried not to notice how much her hands shook. She'd gone out of her way to avoid Caine since their kiss in the foyer, but apparently two days wasn't enough to dampen the memory. Which meant she needed to get her first candidate down here sooner, rather than later.

Because it had been difficult *not* to search him out last night. Especially when she'd accidentally-on-purpose picked a room to do her work in that overlooked the massive drive-way. When his headlights had cut through the darkness, her traitorous heart actually skipped a beat. She'd had a white-knuckle grip on her papers as she'd listened to his footsteps echo over the tiled floors. Part of her had wanted *him* to search her out, and she'd wanted that desperately.

But he'd given her space, or whatever he'd been trying to accomplish. It should have filled her with relief that she wasn't going to spend any more time than necessary in his unnerving presence, but the emotion clogging the back of her throat wasn't relief.

It was disappointment.

"Damn it." She paced a quick circle around the room and dropped back into the love seat where she'd set up her command central. "Focus on the match. The sooner you get him set up with someone else, the sooner you can go home."

Home to her empty apartment and half-dead fern. She used to love her cozy little loft in the East Village. It was something she and Aiden had always planned on when they were in high school—a loft in the colorful part of the city where there was always something going on at any hour of the day. The perfect place to live life to the fullest and try new experiences. They were going to have countless adventures. The kinds they told their grandchildren about.

But there were no grandchildren. No *children*. No adventures. The ink on their home contract had barely dried when Aiden was gunned down in combat in Afghanistan, leaving her a twenty-one-year-old widow. She hadn't had a chance to truly start living before it was all taken away.

Addison sighed. Life could be cruel sometimes. She'd moved on, and thrown herself into helping people find the one thing she'd never have again. Gollum must have sensed her spiraling mood, because the dog trotted over and laid her head on Addison's lap. She absently petted the white fur. "It's okay, girl. I'm just being melodramatic."

Because the truth was that helping other people find their soul mates didn't fulfill her like it used to. She used to be able to almost—*almost*—feel what they felt as they went through the first steps of falling in love. But she hadn't had that fluttering feeling in her stomach for a long time now.

Until Caine.

The problem was *he* gave her the fluttery feeling. The last person who affected her so completely was *Aiden*. It didn't make any sense. People only got one chance at their soul mate. One try and if it ended early, at least they were blessed enough to have felt that all-encompassing love for even a short time.

There were no second chances.

Hadn't Grandmother told her that over and over again as she was growing up? Her grandparents had had a love story for the ages—meeting on the cusp of World War II when her grandmother was a nurse and her grandfather was a pilot. After a whirlwind courtship and quick marriage, they spent years apart exchanging some of the most romantic letters Addison had ever read. And when the war was done, they had ten years together full of joy and children before her grandfather passed away of a heart attack, leaving Grandmother as a widow and mother of three at thirty-five.

She could still remember sitting on her grandmother's knee and listening to the story, the smell of cookies baking in the oven and the chimes softly ringing on the front porch. *Plenty of people thought I should remarry and give a father to your mother and uncles, but I told them the same thing I'm telling you—John was my soul mate. He was the love of my life, and you only get one of those. To marry someone else would be a betrayal to that and to the poor man who put a ring on my finger.*

Grandmother had turned ninety this year and she still got that sad smile on her face when she talked about her soul mate.

"God, I *am* a downer today." She nudged Gollum's head

off her thigh and pulled her computer into her lap. She already had the eight profiles up, so it was a matter of setting them side-by-side. As promised, all were beautiful and all were successful in their own right. They ranged from blond to brunette to redhead, so there should be something to his taste no matter what it was.

Her skin heated as his voice coursed through her memory. *I seem to have developed a keen fascination with redheads.* He'd been trying to make her uncomfortable. She had to keep that in the front of her mind, because she wasn't reacting to him like she usually would with a pushy alpha male. Normally, it'd be easy to put on the cold front and shove him back to where he belonged. She'd never had to worry about *her* losing control before.

It wasn't a comforting thought.

Giving up work for the time being, she kicked off her shoes and went to sit on the floor in the midst of Gollum's pups. They each had very a distinct personality and she'd privately dubbed them after the Ninja Turtles after she found them digging a pizza out of Caine's trash can yesterday morning. It was silly, but the names fit in their own way. Mikey was a goofball who could barely walk without tripping over his wide little paws, Leo always seemed to be leading them into mischief, and Donnie was already too smart for his own good. Raph... She leaned over and tapped the floor. As usual, he was sitting back and watching his siblings play rough-and-tumble. "Come here, fella."

He reluctantly made his way over and sniffed her fingers, which the other three took as an invitation to play. They piled into her lap, wiggling and yipping and generally being so cute she wanted to take them all home with her when she left. Addison laughed and played with them, letting her stress melt away. There wasn't much that could worry her in the face of so much puppy love.

"Is puppy the new black?"

She screamed, scaring the pups so badly they all started barking. Gollum moved before she could, knocking her to the ground and standing over her and the puppies. Masculine laughter rocked the room—or maybe that was just Addison's heart. She shoved her hair out of her face and then had to part Gollum's dreads to see Caine. "What are you doing here?"

"I live here."

Why did he always have to be so difficult? "It's not even dark yet. Why are you home?"

"I reckon I can come and go as I please, seeing as how I own the place." He eyed the dog nearly pinning her to the ground. "How exactly are you going to convince some poor, unsuspecting woman that I actually own this dog when it— *she*—looks ready to take a chunk out of me every time I get too close?"

"You—" Having this conversation with the dog in question on her wasn't really a good way to make her point. She wiggled out from beneath Gollum, praying the dog didn't decide to just lie on top of her and hold her in place. It took a little longer than she'd have liked because she didn't want to crush whichever puppy was halfway beneath her hip. Talk about undignified.

Addison got to her knees and had to shove her hair out of her face again. Wonderful. "If you weren't skulking about, she wouldn't feel the need to defend her territory."

"One, I don't skulk anywhere. Two, how many times do I

have to explain that this is *my* territory? She's the newcomer."

"Feel free to tell her that." Her gaze landed on one of the puppies starting to squat. "Raphael, don't you dare!" She lurched to her feet, scooped him up, and ran for the door. Thank God she'd picked a room with easy access to the backyard. Once she'd deposited the puppy outside, she left him to do his business.

"Raphael." Caine's mouth twitched like he was trying to hold back a laugh. "What are the other fluff balls' names?"

She really, really didn't want to tell him. But from the look on his face, she wasn't getting out of this even if she tried to change the subject. "Michelangelo, Donatello, and Leonardo."

The muscle in his cheek starting jumping faster. "Did you name them after Renaissance painters or the Ninja Turtles?"

Would she save face if she claimed the former? She started to do just that, but she couldn't lie under the weight of those gray eyes. "The Ninja Turtles."

"Whose mother is Gollum."

It sounded particularly ridiculous coming out of his mouth. She raised her chin, determined not to feel stupid— and failing. "It fits."

"Oh, I have no doubt." He took the love seat. She tensed when he glanced at her computer, and then felt even more foolish. What was she going to do? Run over there and grab it out of his hands if he decided to snoop? The women he'd see were ones she was considering flying down here to meet him, so trying to keep them from him didn't make any sense.

Flustered and hating that he made her feel that way without actually doing anything, she set about trying to smooth the wrinkles out of her dress. It didn't work. No

matter how hard she ran her hands over the fabric, the
wrinkles jumped back into evidence. Addison had no idea
how long she'd been rubbing at herself when he cleared his
throat. "Tell me about this first woman."

He kept flip-flopping between being a control freak and
not having enough time to actually deal with the tasks she
set for him. It was enough to give her whiplash. "I already
went into this on the phone. You didn't give me a lot to work
with."

"And I'm not judging. I'm asking what it was about her
that made you pick her for me."

She hesitated, but there was nothing on his face but
genuine curiosity. Since he was apparently ready to let the
dog names go without poking at her further, she decided
to answer the question. "I'm trying to develop a baseline,
though I certainly hope you connect with someone as quickly as possible." The words tasted flat, but she charged on,
determined to ignore the niggling worry in her stomach that
she was somehow screwing this up. "Your first date is Sarah
Roberts, a CFO for Free Thinking Inc. She was listed as one
of New York's most powerful women under thirty." And
she was one of Addison's problem clients. The woman was
capable enough, but she had a list of her future husband's
necessary traits as long as her arm. The only reason she'd
considered Sarah at all was that Caine matched nearly 75
percent of them and that was a hell of a lot better than the
other men Addison had tried to push her toward. Even as
picky as she was, Sarah had been excited at the prospect of
meeting him when they talked yesterday.

Then again, who wouldn't want to meet him? He was
gorgeous and successful and had a sterling reputation. If

he was also an overbearing ass, well, that shouldn't surprise anyone.

"Sounds promising." And he didn't sound the least bit interested. "Though that doesn't tell me a damn thing about her."

She froze. "What?"

"You just recited her job and that she's beautiful. Why did you pick her for *me*?"

God, she just wanted to smack him in the face. And then kiss him. It was that impulse more than anything else that had her backing out of the room. "You'll see for yourself when you meet her. Please let Raphael back in when he's done." Needing space, she turned and marched out of the room. But she didn't march fast enough.

"You don't have to run from me, darlin'. I already promised to keep my hands to myself. Unless you're feeling a bit out of control right around now?"

The only way she could prove him wrong was to go back into that room, and she couldn't trust herself to do that because they'd keep arguing and then she'd get so angry, she'd do something she was bound to regret. Even knowing that, it still took more effort than she liked for her to keep walking.

Chapter Seven

"You can't wear that."

Caine gritted his teeth. When Addison said she wanted to look him over before he left for this date, he'd thought it was a great opportunity to see how her resolve to keep away from him was holding. He hadn't expected her to critique him like he was about to take a girl to prom. "What's wrong with what I'm wearing?"

"What *isn't* wrong with it?" She waved a hand at his chest. "You look like you just came in from the office."

"Because I did just come in from the office."

"It's telling her that she's not worth the effort. That's unacceptable."

What was unacceptable was this little redhead playing havoc on his life. He was an idiot for not putting her on a plane home at the first available opportunity, and now he was paying the price. "This is a thousand-dollar suit."

"Is that supposed to impress me? It's sure as hell not

going to impress Sarah Roberts." She propped her hands on her hips. "Don't move. I'll figure out something." Then she hurried up the stairs.

Stay here while she rummaged through his things? Caine didn't think so. He followed, but at a distance, curious as to if she'd actually go into his space. By the time he reached the hallway in his wing of the house, he had his answer. How the hell did she even know where his room was?

Shelving that question for the time being, he stopped just inside the doorway to his suite. Where was... The sight of Addison bent over, her dress riding up the back of her thighs, kicked him in the chest like a draft horse. The temptation to cross the distance between them and help the hem along up over her ass, baring her to him, was nearly too much to take.

No, damn it. He'd said he wouldn't touch her until she kissed him first, and he damn well wasn't going to break his word. No matter how tempting Addison was.

Oblivious, she straightened and held up a shirt he'd forgotten he had. It was what a generous man would call plum. Caine preferred purple. "Absolutely not."

"All you wear is shades of gray."

"There's nothing wrong with gray." The absurdity of defending his clothing choice wasn't lost on him, but apparently she wasn't going to back down.

"Maybe not, but I can already tell you what she'll think if you show up in that. That you're boring. Or, worse, that you think you're Mr. Grey."

"Who?"

She frowned. "As in *Fifty Shades of.*"

"I have no idea what you're talking about."

Her jaw dropped. "Have you been living in a hole for the last three years? You know what, don't bother. I already know the answer to that, but I can't fix a lifetime's worth of issues in a few days. So put on the damn shirt."

Lust curled in his stomach, already fanned into being just by standing in the same room as her. He shouldn't find her so damn hot when she was bossing him around, but Caine couldn't help it. The exasperated look on her face was too much to resist. Holding her gaze, he started unbuttoning his shirt.

Her brown eyes went wide. "What are you doing?"

"Following orders. You told me to change my shirt."

"Not in front of me!"

"Why not? Does it bother you?" He shrugged the shirt off. With her gaze fastened to his chest, she held out the purple shirt, angling her body away from his. He took his time pulling it on, though he had to keep reminding himself that he couldn't follow through on the desire on her face. Not until she made the first move. His cock wasn't listening, though. She was staring at him so intently, he could almost feel it on his skin.

His control held until she *whimpered*.

He wasn't sure what happened. One second he was standing a few feet from her. The next he was in front of her, his hands in her hair and his mouth on hers. He wanted to taste that whimper. Addison's hands instantly went around his back, stroking up his spine as she arched into him. Her tongue met his, the taste of her even better than he remembered. Caine pulled her tighter against him, stroking down her sides and hiking up the hem of her dress until he could cup her ass. She wore some sort of lace panties, but he couldn't tear his mouth from hers to get a better look.

When he started backing her toward the bed, she jerked back. Not all the way back, though. Her hands didn't leave his chest. "God, stop."

"Why? You want me as much as I want you."

"I don't do this."

"Darlin', maybe you never have before, but you are with me."

For some reason, that seemed to scare the shit out of her. She took another step back, wobbling a little in her heels, her hands leaving his skin almost in slow motion, until she only touched him with her fingertips, and then finally not at all. "No, I'm not doing anything. *We're* not doing anything." She glanced at the clock next to his bed. "And if you don't leave now, you're going to be late. Sarah doesn't like to be kept waiting." Then she was gone, leaving him with a raging hard-on and a hell of a lot of confusion.

Because she wanted him. She wouldn't practically climb him like a tree every time he kissed her if she didn't. It might have been quite a while since Caine had anything that could be termed a fling, but he wasn't misreading the signals. Which left the question... Why was she fighting it so hard? Was it purely because of professional purposes, or was there something else going on?

He finished dressing while he mulled it over, and then headed for his car. Addison had thrown a fit over the Jaguar, so he'd had the Cadillac brought out. Since she didn't appear to yell at him over how ostentatious it was, he figured it got her seal of approval. He waited until he was out of the driveway before calling his little brother. The phone barely rang twice before Brock answered, "I told her it was a bad idea, but you know how Regan is. She gets her mind set on something and it takes a brick wall and a pile of dynamite to deter her."

"It's fine."

Brock was silent for a beat. "You're taking this well— *too* well. What's going on?"

Fuck if he knew. There was something about the woman that drove him crazy, and made him want more of her all at the same time. It didn't make a lick of sense. "I'm not sure yet."

"Do you want me to call Addison off? She's a nice girl, but she gets as stubborn as Regan when her eye is on the prize. If she's making your life a living hell—"

"She's a pain in the ass, but I'm not ready to send her home yet. Is your wife around?"

Another beat of silence. "Sure, she's right here." A rustling on his end of the phone and then Regan was there, sounding entirely too chipper. "Hey, Caine. How's the wife search going?"

He heard Brock cursing in the background and had to laugh. "You have no shame, do you?"

"Not when I'm right."

"Are you ever wrong?"

"It's happened once or twice. Not this time, though."

That remained to be seen. "What's Addison's story?"

He could almost feel her attention sharpening. "Does it matter?"

"You sent her here, Regan. The least you can do is answer my damn question." Because it *did* matter. There was more to the woman than the steamrolling matchmaker. He'd seen her with his nieces, seen the bittersweet expression on her face. That came from somewhere, and Addison wasn't about to share. He wanted to know more about her, but she shut him down every time he pushed. So he'd go around her.

"She's a hell of a matchmaker, though she doesn't date. She was married to her high school sweetheart, but he got himself killed in Afghanistan three years in." Regan paused. "Addison is a big believer in soul mates."

"She's mentioned it."

"No, you don't get it. She thinks each person only gets one. As far as she's concerned, Aiden was hers and that's all she wrote."

Caine turned onto the street Jean Claude's was on. "So that's it for her? She never dated after this guy died?"

"You're awfully curious about someone who's down there solely to set you up with other women."

It wouldn't be a good idea to let Regan know just how twisted up his intentions were when it came to Addison. Hell, *he* still wasn't sure what he intended. "We'll talk about the fact that you sent a matchmaker down here without my permission later."

He was about to hang up when she spoke. "Caine, you're family now and Brock loves the hell out of you, but if you hurt Addison, I will ruin you." The threat should have sounded dramatic and unrealistic, but the intent in her voice sent a chill down his spine. Regan meant it. If she decided she didn't like the outcome of whatever this thing with Addison was, she'd put all her considerable resources into bringing him down. As CEO of McNeill Enterprises, he should be damn near untouchable, but he wasn't about start placing bets when it came to Regan.

It was a good thing he had no intention of hurting Addison.

"I'll take that into consideration."

"Caine—"

He hung up. She hadn't given him a lot, but it was something to think about. He handed his keys to the valet and headed into the restaurant. The hostess smiled at him. "Mr. McNeill. Your date is already here. This way, please."

He followed the hostess through an assortment of tables toward the back of the room. When he conducted business dinners, this was where he always worked. Apparently Addison had been busy meddling with the reservation just like she was meddling with the rest of his life. The woman at the corner table stood, and he got his first glimpse of her— tall and blond and as beautiful as Addison had promised.

Then Sarah Roberts opened her mouth. "You're late."

Christ, it was going to be a long date.

• • •

Addison paced in what had quickly become her working room in Caine's house. It was a sitting room with comfortable floral chairs and wispy lace curtains that gave a perfect view of the driveway. She could all too easily imagine Southern ladies lounging here, sipping tea and gossiping.

He'd been gone only an hour, but that was plenty of time to mentally flog herself. What was she thinking, letting him kiss her again? As soon as he touched her, she should have shoved him on his ass and coldly informed him that she wasn't interested. Not clung to him like she couldn't get enough. Because that's what it'd felt like—she was starving and he was a giant banquet laid out in her honor.

Caine wasn't hers. It didn't matter how good it felt when

he touched her, or how painfully perfect his body was. He belonged to his soul mate, and that wasn't Addison.

Was it Sarah Roberts?

She turned another circuit. Sarah very well could be. She was successful and cultured and brought a lot to the table. Would Caine kiss her the same way he'd kissed Addison? Would he run those big hands down her back and cup her ass so he could grind himself against her? Would he…

"Gah!" She kicked off her heels. "This isn't doing anything but driving me crazy."

Needing a distraction, she worked her way through the halls until she found the room she'd spied during her earlier exploration. It was dominated by an immaculate baby grand, and it had been calling to her since she discovered it. She traced a single finger over the keys, but her nerves were strung too tightly to sit down and play anything.

Her phone rang and she startled so badly, she almost dropped it. Maybe there was some emergency back in NYC that would get her mind off the emergency this situation down here had become. There had to be *some* kind of fire she was required to put out so she wouldn't have to think about his hands on Sarah. "Addison St. Claire."

"Are you mad at me?"

Her knees buckled at the sound of Caine growling in her ear and she dropped onto the love seat. *Get it together.* She cleared her throat. "What?"

"You must be mad at me. That's the only logical conclusion as to why you'd force me on a date with this woman."

That got her head in the game. "Where is she?" Was he saying this right in front of Sarah? She wouldn't put it past him. Sarah would never forgive her for witnessing her humiliation.

"In the bathroom. Christ, darlin', I'm not a total dickwad."

Thank God. That worry out of the way, she could focus on the next problem. "Why the hell are you calling me in the middle of your date?"

"Because it's a disaster. She's a— Shit, she's back." And then the bastard hung up.

Addison stared at her phone. She looked at Gollum, who had taken up a spot safely out of the path of her pacing. "He hung up on me." And worse, he'd called her in the middle of the date. She ignored the tiny trickle of relief at knowing the date was going horribly, and focused on what the next step had to be, because the only other option was to drive down there and smack some sense into him. Work. Yes, work was the answer. She flipped through her list of potential matches, but it was impossible to pick the next one without knowing what had gone wrong with Sarah.

She'd just started pacing again when her phone rang again. She slid her thumb to answer it. "What the hell is wrong with you?"

"Addison?"

Her stomach dropped. It wasn't Caine. No, there was only one perfectly distinguished woman who'd be calling her right now. She took a deep breath and tried to force some cheer into her voice. "Sarah?"

"Addison, what were you thinking making me come all this way for that man? He's horrid."

She might have said something very similar recently, but she couldn't stop herself from defending him. "He's nearly exactly what you asked for, Sarah. The only aspect of your list that he didn't fit was his location."

"That might be so, but he was so dreadfully *dull*. All we did was talk business. If I wanted to talk business, I could have stayed in New York and talked to the countless men I work with."

Dull? Caine might be a lot of things, but dull didn't make the top ten—or even the top one hundred.

The match might be a disaster, but maybe she could use it to finally open Sarah's eyes. "Does this mean you'll finally listen to some of my suggestions about figuring out what you absolutely won't compromise on? I've given you exactly what you wanted, and it sounds like it's not melding well."

Sarah sighed. "Fine, Addison. Have it your way. Just get me out of the godforsaken South as soon as possible."

That, she could do. "I have you on a flight out tomorrow morning."

"Thank God. You've emailed me the details?"

"Of course."

"Thank you." Then she was gone, leaving Addison to figure out how to handle the other half of the date. It might not be fair to blame this whole thing on Caine, but it was easier to do that than to think that maybe that ill-advised kiss before he left was part of the problem.

"It won't happen again. I won't let it." But she'd said the very same thing before, and look how well *that* had worked out. She obviously couldn't be trusted to avoid the temptation that was Caine McNeill. Maybe it would be better if she wasn't actually living in his house, but going to a hotel meant she'd have to drive here every day to muscle him into being more approachable.

Obviously she'd failed this time.

The front door slammed hard enough to shake the entire

house. Gollum growled, but apparently she'd gotten used to Caine enough to know she didn't need to defend her babies when he was around. Addison took one look at the scattered evidence of her state of mind and decided that having him in what had become her space wasn't the best plan. So she marched toward the door, deciding to meet him in the formal dining room.

The massive wooden table looked solid enough to have survived the Civil War and a few others, all without losing its perfection and charm. It was polished within an inch of its life, as were the dozen sturdy chairs around it, as if a dinner party were just minutes away.

Apparently the staff he'd hired to keep this place clean lived in hope.

Caine shoved through the door, looking a little wild, his hair standing on end as if he'd been running his hands through it, and his gray eyes darker than normal. His gaze raked her from head to toe, and Addison had half a second to regret the comfortable drawstring pants and wish she had a bra on under her tank top. *This* was why living under the same roof as him was a terrible idea.

He stalked toward her. "If that's the best woman you can come up with, your so-called matchmaking skills are seriously lacking."

Instinct demanded she retreat, but her feet stayed firmly planted. "There's only so much I can do. You have to be able to fly on your own."

"That's the thing. I was flying just fine on my own before you showed up." He sliced a hand through the air when she opened her mouth to respond. "I already know your opinion on that. I don't need to hear it again."

Well, that was too damn bad. "What possessed you to talk about business on a date?"

He stopped just out of reach, which was a good thing, because she didn't know what to do with this less-than-poised Caine. "What else was I supposed to talk about? She was curt to the point of being rude when I tried to make small talk, and all I could think about was how I could still taste you on my lips."

Chapter Eight

Caine couldn't remember the last time he felt so out of control. Maybe it had never happened. All he knew was that he'd sat across the table from that beautiful blonde and realized that she was exactly the sort of thing his father would approve of, to the point where Caine could almost see his old man checking traits of an approved wife off his list.

And he'd felt nothing. Less than nothing.

Sarah Roberts bored him, and the thought of spending the rest of his life with someone like that left him feeling like he had been in a free fall for the last thirty-five years and was only just now waking up.

The only thing that wasn't directly connected was Addison.

And now she stood there, staring at him as if he were crazed. Hell, maybe he was. He certainly felt like it.

"Caine, what happened before—"

"I'm tired of talking." He pulled her into his arms and kissed her, taking her mouth just like he had earlier tonight.

He actually tasted her breath of indecision before she melted against him, her hands sliding up his chest to tangle in his hair. Christ, the woman tasted better than the bottle of '88 Le Pin he had in the wine cellar. He kicked the closest chair to the side and lifted her onto the table. The new position lined their bodies up perfectly, and he couldn't help the growl that rose in his chest at the feeling of her legs wrapping around his waist. He broke the kiss and leaned his forehead against hers. "Let me take care of you, darlin'. Please."

Her body went taut, and he held his breath, sure that she'd push him away just like she had every time before. "Okay."

The word came out so small, he was sure he'd heard wrong. Caine lifted his head so he could see her face. For the first time since they met, she actually looked unsure of herself. It was enough to make him wonder if Regan was right and she hadn't let another man this close since her husband died. The thought of being the first...

The possessive feeling that surged had him clenching his hands in an effort to keep from hauling her ass into his bed and ruining her for any other man. It wasn't rational and it sure as fuck wasn't sane, but the desire was there all the same.

But that wasn't what tonight was about. It was about *her*. Because if the shitty date had made anything clear, it was that there was only one woman who made him feel alive and it was the pain-in-the-ass matchmaker who was currently overhauling his life.

So he had to make her want him as much.

Caine grinned, liking the way she shivered when he did. He could already see the wheels in her head trying to turn, to convince her that this was a mistake. If he let her think long enough, she'd find a reason to stop this. So he kissed her again, stroking her tongue with his until she writhed against him. He hooked his thumbs under the bottom of her tank top and peeled it up her body, breaking the kiss long enough to pull it over her head. Unable to resist, he moved back just enough so that he could look at her. "Fuck."

Her pale skin was completely unmarred by tan lines, long neck leading the eye south to her perfect breasts, each topped with a rosy nipple practically begging for his mouth. He kissed his way down her neck to answer the siren call, moving slowly, following the urging of her fingers in his hair. She smelled faintly of a sweet sea breeze, so good it made him groan. Was there anything about this woman that didn't do it for him?

He took her nipple in his mouth, rolling his tongue over the bud, and Addison nearly shot off the table. "God!" Her grip on his hair was nearly painful, but he relished every pull because she was the one doing it. *He* was doing this to her, pushing her past the point of control.

Savage satisfaction filled him as he moved to her other nipple, giving it the same treatment. He leaned her back on the table until she lay flat, lashing her with his tongue until her entire body shook, pulled so taut it was a wonder she didn't break into a million pieces.

And he wasn't done yet. Not by a long shot.

He undid the drawstring on her pants and pulled them off, leaving her in only a pair of lace bikini-style panties. They were a pale rose—exactly the same shade as her nipples. She lifted her head, her eyes wild as he dropped the pants on the floor next to him. There was desire there, but also a thread of fear. He ran his hands up the outside of her thighs to cup her hips. "The panties stay on, darlin.'"

When she didn't respond, aside from the little tremors of her body, he stopped the little circular movement he'd been stroking on her skin. "Do you want me to stop?"

She searched his face. "The panties stay on?"

The sheer amount of trust she was putting in him to keep his word staggered Caine. He'd die before he broke it. He met her gaze. "I promise."

Addison let her head drop back to the table. "Don't stop."

He hadn't realized how tense he'd been as he waited for her answer until his legs threatened to give out. Caine pressed a kiss to the inside of her knee. "I won't." He reached behind him for the chair he'd kicked aside and dragged it back so he could sit down. Having her laid out like the best kind of feast did things for him—things he wasn't completely prepared to deal with. Because she trusted him to take this further without pushing it too far, and he fully intended to reward that trust.

He pulled her to the edge of the table and stroked his hands over her hip bones and down to trace over the lace of her panties. He teased her, dipping one finger just beneath the edge of the fabric, silently letting her know that he could keep this up all night if he were so inclined.

He wasn't.

She lifted her hips as his finger continued its journey, stopping just to the side of her center. "Please, Caine. I don't think I can stand it if you keep teasing me."

Hell, he'd barely started. But he couldn't ignore the desperation in her voice any more than he could ignore how soaked her panties were. He slipped his hand beneath the fabric, pushing them to the side so he had free access to her body. She whimpered as he spread her wetness around, before he pushed one finger into her slowly, nearly cursing again at how tight she was. And then her hands were in his hair again, silently demanding what he was only too happy to give.

He lowered his head and kissed her through the lace as he worked her with his finger. That first stroke of his tongue was pure heaven, and her crying out was music to his ears. But he wanted her with no barriers between them, so he used his free hand to drag the fabric farther to the side. She arched up to meet each plunge of his finger, her body already tightening around him. She had to be close, and he was the one bringing her to the edge.

Caine almost pulled back, almost kept on teasing her, but then he remembered the desperation in her voice. If she really hadn't had this with anyone in years, then he sure as fuck wasn't going to deny her now. Still, he couldn't help lifting his head and looking up her body. He wanted her to know exactly whose hands were on her. "I'm going to let you come, and when I do, you're going to be calling my name to the heavens. Got it?"

"Yes, yes, whatever you want, just please don't stop." The words came out almost as a sob.

"I won't, darlin.'" He covered her clit with his mouth, flicking his tongue over the sensitive nub as he pushed a second finger into her.

She lasted until the third stroke. "*Caine.*"

He leaned his forehead against her lower stomach, doing his damnedest to remember why he couldn't bury his cock inside her right this second. *You promised, you shit.* Yeah, that was it. He couldn't resist licking her again, though, to tease out a few more of those delicious cries.

He drew back, breathing as hard as she was, his control damn near to the breaking point. If she'd reached for him, he would have been on her in a second. But Addison blinked at him as if slowly coming back to herself. Then she smiled, the sweetest, most trusting expression anyone had ever turned his way.

Christ. He had to get her out of here before he lost it, but he couldn't just leave her like this, not after what they'd just shared. So he stood, paused to adjust his pants, and scooped her into his arms. She leaned her head against his shoulder. "You don't have to carry me. I could probably walk...in like twenty minutes."

Because of *him*. He held her tighter as he started for the stairs. "I promised I'd take care of you."

"I think you more than managed that." Her eyes drifted shut.

If he were a smart man, he would have left her on that table and walked away. But he obviously had lost what common sense he possessed because he carried her up to the room she'd picked for herself. It was the pink suite, one that had been empty for as long as he could remember. In a house of boys, there wasn't a lot of use for a room that seemed designed for a princess. It fit Addison, though, and he liked seeing evidence of her settling in scattered on the dresser and nightstand.

He set her on the bed and pulled the covers up to her shoulders. She looked smaller in the massive king-size bed. Delicate. It made him want to take her to *his* bed so he could make sure she didn't break, but that was a terrible idea. If she was in his bed... Yeah, better that she stayed here. He moved to the door and glanced back, but she seemed to have already fallen asleep. "Good night, Addison."

As he made his way to his own room, he came to one painful conclusion. He was well and truly fucked when it came to Addison St. Claire.

Chapter Nine

Addison opened her eyes as soon as the morning sun hit her face. One glance at the clock confirmed that it was well past when she should have been awake. The only upside to sleeping in was that Caine must already be gone for work.

Caine.

She could feel a freak-out pending, but for once in her life, she pushed it away. Right now all she wanted to do was luxuriate in how good her body felt after what he'd done to her last night.

It had been years since she let someone close enough to touch her like that—ever since Lee, her friend who'd thought he could help her recover from the death of her husband and be her everything. Lee had been as perfect as a man could be—sweet, and strong, and loving—and he hadn't done a single thing for her. It didn't make any sense. Those were the qualities in Aiden that had made her heart speed up, but with Lee, she had to force herself to respond.

And when even that didn't work, she *faked* it.

It was then that she'd finally had to face the facts—her grandmother was right. Everyone had one soul mate, and she'd lost hers forever. Addison rolled over and stretched. Last night hadn't been sweet, not by a long shot. Caine had kissed her like he was never going to stop, and then he'd gone and done things to her body that had her shaking and fighting to not beg him to take it all the way. She hadn't faked a single damn thing.

And he'd kept his word.

The sad fact was that if he'd looked at her sideways after that orgasm-to-end-all-orgasms, she would have done anything he wanted. More than that, *she* wanted. If he could make her feel so damn good with only his hands and mouth, how much better would it be if his whole body was involved? Even thinking about it made her shiver all over again.

Except he hadn't looked at her sideways. He hadn't taken advantage of the desire that turned her common sense inside out. He hadn't even taken off her panties. All because he'd promised.

She didn't know what to do with that.

No, that wasn't true. She knew *exactly* what she wanted to do with Caine, which was the problem. Right now she had a choice—she could keep silently freaking out, or she could do something about it. Her traitorous brain offered up all sorts of scenarios that involved doing something with him, but she forcibly silenced it. She was not, under any circumstances, going to offer herself up for another round as soon as he got home. The fact that she wanted to so much was a problem, because she couldn't pretend anymore that this thing with him wasn't going to happen again—and escalate next time it did.

Which meant she had to get him matched sooner, rather than later.

The thought hurt, but she pushed that feeling away, too. This was sheer self-preservation, and she'd be a fool to give in to her desire for him. Doing that would lead to ruin for both of them.

Taking a deep breath, she started poking at the problem. Sarah was too uptight for him, which really meant she was too much *like* Caine. So he'd need someone who was a free thinker, someone who'd challenge him and expand his horizons. It'd be good for him, no matter how much he might initially hate it.

Addison stretched one last time and climbed out of bed. She needed her list. There were a couple who'd work, but she needed to find the right one or she'd end up in Caine's bed faster than she could say "clusterfuck."

It was tempting to make a detour to the massive kitchen and see if she could scrounge up some food, but she recognized it for the stalling tactic it was. *That* got her moving. She made her way to the room where she'd set up shop and froze at the sight of the cheery pink sticky note on top of her computer. It definitely hadn't been there when she left the room last night.

She approached it like she would a snake, ready to spring back at the least provocation. Even as she did it, she recognized she was being completely irrational. It was just a sticky piece of paper. It couldn't hurt her. But that didn't stop adrenaline from pumping through her body as she stopped close enough to read the chicken scratch.

See you tonight.

No signature, but he didn't really need one, did he? She peeled it off the computer and stared hard. He had to be feeling pretty damn cocky right now. He'd gotten what he wanted, and he had to know exactly how twisted up she'd be over what they'd done. This was both a promise and a threat.

She couldn't make herself throw it away, so she pressed it to the inside of the cover of the thriller she'd been slowly picking away at for the last few days. Then she opened her computer and tried not to panic. She had to get someone down here, and it had to be tonight. The alternative was too dangerous to consider.

A name practically jumped out at her as she scanned the list she'd made up. Rachel Hamilton. She remembered Rachel. The woman was a new client, barely with them two weeks, and she'd made a big impression when Addison interviewed her. She was a web designer and so peppy and sweet, it would take a meaner man than Caine to shut her down. In short, she was perfect.

She checked the time—early, but not too early for a phone call—and dialed. If she remembered correctly, Rachel was a night owl, but she should still be up by now. Hopefully. The phone barely rang twice when she answered, "Addison! It's good to hear from you."

It was like this with her every time they talked. She was the kind of person who'd never met a stranger, and Addison was pretty sure she could charm the birds from the trees if she ever tried. Caine wouldn't know what hit him. Her chest panged at the thought, but she forced a smile into her voice. "I think I've found a man that might interest you."

"Wow, that was fast. I'm in."

She'd thought Rachel would say that. "Then I have a question for you... How do you feel about Tennessee?"

. . .

Caine got home, expecting to spend an evening slowly seducing Addison. What he met was chaos as soon as he walked through the door. He stopped to avoid getting run over by his woman with a phone, and then could only stare as Gollum trotted by, followed by her four pups. Sometime during the day, they had acquired collars, and he couldn't help the small smile as he took in the colors—red, orange, blue, and purple. He'd bet they corresponded with their names. He started to greet Addison, but she held up a finger and turned away, still issuing instructions to whoever was on the other side of the phone call—something about a car pickup.

He crossed his arms over his chest and waited. Something was going on, and he wanted to know what. Though he had his suspicions. He'd thought that restraining himself last night would be enough to set them in the right direction, but apparently he'd been wrong. She was still going forward with her plan to match him with someone else.

She hung up the phone and spun on her heel, nearly running him over before she realized he wasn't moving. "What are you doing still standing here? Go change."

Damn it, he'd really hoped he wasn't right. "Why do I need to change?"

"Because you're almost late." She glanced at her watch. "Correction, you *are* late. So please hurry."

He wanted to shake her until she snapped out of the

denial she seemed content to cloak herself in, but he suspected that would only make her dig in her heels harder. Caine turned away and stalked up the stairs, considering his next move. He couldn't let this stand. None of these dates were going to succeed, because there was only one woman he was interested in. He grabbed the first colored shirt he found—a deep blue one—and shrugged it on. She wanted him to go on a date? Well, he'd damn well do just that.

But he wasn't going alone.

By the time he made it back to the foyer, Addison was a mass of frantic energy, practically bouncing in place. She barely gave him a once-over before she opened the front door. "Try not to bore this one. She's a nice lady."

Caine stopped just this side of the threshold. "I make no promises."

"Wait—what? Why would you say that?"

Because he was pissed, and growing more so by the second. "Well, you know me. I'm dull as a box of rocks. I'll probably tell her about the new project set to break ground this spring. I'm sure she'll like that."

"You can't!" She looked like she wanted to kick him in the shins. "Good God, this isn't going to work if you're not putting forth at least a little effort. I can't do everything."

"Then you should be there with me."

Her gaze snapped back to him. "What?"

"I'm not getting in that goddamn car unless you're coming along." If she thought he was bluffing, she had another think coming. He wanted *her*, not some mystery woman she was sure was perfect for him. Would this new woman charge into his life and challenge him on a daily basis? He doubted it.

But the only way he could get Addison to see what a mistake this was would be for her to literally *see* it.

She shook her head. "I'm not going on a date with you and Rachel. What if you hit it off? Am I supposed to sit in the backseat as chaperone?" Something flickered through her eyes—*jealousy*—and he knew he had her.

"Of course not." He wasn't taking this other woman anywhere. "I'd call you a cab."

There it was again. She didn't like the idea of him with another woman any more than he did. "This is unacceptable."

"It's a shame she flew all the way down here for nothing."

"You're impossible. Fine. I'll go to the restaurant, but that's it. Get your ass in the car." She grabbed his arm and towed him down the steps to where his Cadillac waited. She *had* been busy. When he held the door for her, she huffed out a breath and climbed into the passenger seat. It was everything he could do not to slam the door. Stubborn, idiotic woman.

"Now, I need you to remember…" She trailed off when he glared. "Never mind."

They didn't speak the rest of the way to the restaurant. His agitation only grew, no matter how much he tried to get control of it. It wasn't this date's fault that their matchmaker was determined to ignore all sanity and keep trying to set him up. He needed to have his shit together before he met her, because he wasn't asshole enough to be a dick to an innocent.

No matter how angry he was.

The hostess's smile dimmed at the look on his face, so apparently he wasn't doing a great job of keeping his shit together. "I have a reservation. I need *her*"—he pointed at

Addison—"set up in the room next door."

"Sir, I can't really…" She gulped when he shoved two hundreds into her hand. "I'll take care of that immediately."

"Thank you."

Addison spun on him as soon as she disappeared. "You scared her."

"She'll survive."

"I don't know what your problem is, but—"

"You want to know my problem, darlin'?" He stepped into her, so close they almost touched, so close her breath caught and her pupils dilated. "My problem is that a little over twenty-four hours ago, I had you on my table and coming against my mouth. And now you're shoving me at the first available woman you can find."

A throat clearing had him tearing his gaze away from her—a blessing, because if he had another second, he'd kiss her and then it would be all over. The hostess watched them with wide eyes. "I have your rooms ready."

"Thank you." He moved after her, leaving Addison to follow or be left behind. The room contained a single table set for two and was decorated with warm gold and red, the low light designed to flatter. He moved to the adjoining door and opened it in time to see her take a seat.

She immediately jumped to her feet. "Now listen—"

"You can yell at me later." It was far too satisfying to cut her off. "You wouldn't want to interfere with my *date*, would you?"

For a second he thought—hoped—she'd keep going, but she took a deep breath, smoothed down her green dress, and sank gracefully into her seat. "Of course not."

"I thought so." He left the door cracked and moved to

his own seat. The hostess reappeared a few minutes later, this time with a brunette in tow. Caine stood because it was the polite thing to do, and even managed a smile.

She grinned in return, the expression lighting up her face. "I'm Rachel. You must be Caine." She really was a pretty little thing, her brunette hair pulled back into a sleek ponytail that exposed her model-like cheekbones.

"Would you like something to drink?"

"Sure." She sank into the chair he pulled out for her. "Addison was right, you really are gorgeous."

What the hell was he supposed to say to that? "Thank you."

"No, thank you." She laughed. "I'm sorry. She told me not to be too forward, but I don't get to interact with people face-to-face all that often, so I'm out of practice. And really, what's the point in pretending I'm suave and polished? If we spend any amount together, you'll figure it out for a lie, and I'd rather just be honest to begin with."

He laughed. "That's a refreshing way to look at it. And I'm familiar with Addison's pep talks."

"Really?" Rachel leaned forward. It was a move that, on anyone else, he'd suspect was meant to draw his eye down the long line of her body, but she seemed completely oblivious to her charm. "You seem pretty put-together. What could she possibly have to correct you on?"

"Would you like a list?" Had he imagined the huff from the other room? He didn't think so. "Apparently I'm intimidating, and wear too much gray."

"Oh dear. I'd think both those things would be assets."

"That's what I told her. She didn't listen, though. She even bought me a damn dog."

Rachel nodded, the edges of her mouth twitching. "I

have it on good knowledge that chicks dig dogs, so it looks like she was pointing you in the right direction."

"What other pointers did she give you?"

"Oh, not to wear my comic character shirts, or ones that swear, or pretty much anything in my wardrobe. Also, to avoid talking about comics or web design or how Black Widow would totally kick any other Marvel character's ass in a fight." She waved her hand. "So, you know, all the things."

"Sounds like we're both works in progress." He took a pull from his beer. "If anyone else had told me that I'm an ass who can barely dress myself, I would have kicked them to the curb. But she's a force of nature. By the time I realize she's about to rearrange my life, she's already there and doing it." He lowered his voice a little. "To tell you the truth, I'm actually starting to like it—and her."

He heard movement at the door before the woman herself marched into the room. "I'm sorry, Rachel, but this is ridiculous." Addison poked him in the shoulder. "I know what you're doing and I don't appreciate it."

"What I'm doing is having a nice conversation with Rachel."

"Bullshit. You're trying to sabotage this date just like you did the last one, and I won't stand for it."

He took another drink. "What are you going to do about it?"

Rachel's gaze jumped between them. "Uh…do you guys need a minute?"

"No."

"Yes." Caine raised his eyebrows when she turned a dangerous red color. "You're the one barging in here, making a scene. It's not very professional."

"I... You... Ah! I can't deal with you anymore. Sabotage the date for all I care." She strode to the door, but paused in the doorway. "Rachel, I promise I'll make this up to you."

"Make it up to *me*?" She laughed and toasted them with her wine. "This is the most entertainment I've had in months."

At least someone was getting entertained by this mess.

Chapter Ten

What the hell was wrong with her?

Addison burst through the front door and then just stood there, not sure how her life had spun so out of control. Storming in to interrupt a date between two clients? That was a giant no-no, but it seemed like she'd been breaking every single rule she had ever created since she met Caine. Don't kiss clients? Don't let clients stretch you out on their formal dining room table and make you come? Don't fantasize about doing even more with said client?

Yeah, she was failing in a singular fashion.

She needed someone who'd be rational and talk her down. She paced, staring at her phone. Regan was the first person to come to mind, but Regan had also sent her on this mission to begin with. What would her friend think to know she'd been crossing the line with her brother-in-law?

Damn it. It didn't matter. She needed help, and she didn't have anyone else to call. She started to lift her phone and then had to scramble out of the way as the front door slammed open and Caine marched through. She looked behind him, half expecting Rachel to be there, too, but the walkway was empty. "Where's Rachel?" He had to have left minutes after her to get here so quickly.

"I paid for whatever she wanted to eat and drink and left. She seemed to think it was a more than fair trade."

"You are so goddamn rude! You can't just pay for a meal and leave her alone in a strange city by herself. What kind of gentleman does that?"

"The kind who didn't want the date to begin with."

Here they went again. "Caine, I may look like a miracle worker, but even I can't match you up with anyone worthwhile when you're actively working against me." And she *had* to match him up with someone. She just had to.

"Why not you?"

She froze. "What?"

He kicked the door shut. "Why not you? Regardless of what you may think of me, I don't strip women down, make them come, and tuck them into bed just for the hell of it." He closed the distance between them, one purposeful step at a time.

That's what she was afraid of. "It would never work with us."

"How the hell do you know? Do you have a crystal ball stored around here somewhere?"

"Because you only get one soul mate, and I've already had mine."

He stared. "That's the dumbest thing I've ever heard."

"Wow, Caine. Don't hold back. Tell me what you really think."

Had he moved closer? She wasn't sure, but he suddenly seemed to take up entirely too much space. "What I think, darlin', is that you're scared. You loved a man once and losing him shredded you to pieces. How long did it take you to put yourself back together again after he died?"

Years. Years of forcing herself to go through the motions before she started to actually enjoy life again. She bit her lip. "You're missing the point."

"I don't think I am. I'm right on the money." And then he was in front of her, his big hand cupping the side of her face. "And I'm not interested in dating any of these matches. I'm interested in dating *you*."

Before she could come up with a reply—and what was she supposed to say?—he kissed her. It was a long, slow exploration of her mouth, his taste one she couldn't resist if she tried. And she was so damn tired of trying.

Caine lifted his head, but he didn't release his hold on her. "I'm taking you to bed tonight, darlin'."

"And if I don't want to?"

He searched her face. "I'm not going to force you and you damn well know it. You want me to stop, then this stops."

"Just like that?"

"Just like that."

It would be so easy to say the words that would make him back off. So easy to retreat back into her safe place where she didn't have to face the mixture of uncomfortable emotions that rose whenever he touched her. So easy to go back to how things were when she was sure the world fit a certain mold.

She couldn't force the words past her lips. Instead, the ones she gave voice to sealed her fate: "Take me to bed, Caine."

"With pleasure." He scooped her into his arms and started up the staircase. At least he moved fast enough that they were in his bedroom before she had a chance to start second-guessing herself. Or worse, *not* second-guessing herself. She was a hot mess.

He let her slide down his body until she was on her feet again, and then pulled her dress over her head. She went to work on his shirt, unbuttoning it with shaking fingers. The man's chest was criminally good, and if she was doing this, she wanted him as naked as she was about to be.

She was definitely doing this.

The cool air on her skin almost snapped her out of her lustful haze, but Caine stepped into her, his chest pressing against hers, so much skin-on-skin contact that she had to stop him with her hands on his shoulders. "A second. I need a second." And God bless him, he waited for her to adjust. All too soon, that overstimulation turned to just stimulation. She closed her eyes. "Okay, I'm good."

"When was the last time you got this close to a man?"

Years. Years and years and years. She bit her lip, nearly moaning as he ran his hands up her sides and down her back. Just when it seemed like he'd forgotten the question, he stopped at her hips and gave them a slight squeeze. "When, darlin'?"

"Six years ago." It had been a year after Aiden's death, and she'd been so desperate to feel something beyond overwhelming loss that she'd talked herself into bed with Lee. He'd been a shoulder for her to lean on up to that point, and it seemed like things could potentially work. It had been a terrible mistake. All it had done was make her miss Aiden more, and it had cemented her belief that her grandmother had been right all along. She only got one soul mate.

And she wasn't Lee's. He'd met his six months after things exploded between them. Their Christmas card from last year was still on her fridge, the happiness on their faces a reminder of what could go wrong if someone tried to force things.

Was this going to ruin things with Caine? She couldn't decide which answer to that question scared her more.

For his part, he looked shocked. The expression passed, though, replaced by something that made her thighs clench. He looked at her like she was virgin territory that he was about to conquer and claim for his own. The man truly did have a savage streak a mile wide. He clasped the back of her neck and leaned down for a kiss. This one felt different from the others, more like he really *was* claiming her. The sensation was nearly overwhelming, from his tongue stroking hers to his hard body against her own, and she clung to him, shaking.

Caine unhooked her bra with one hand and tossed it aside. He used his grip on her neck to force her to meet his eyes. "Tonight you're mine." Then he released her, the loss of his touch nearly making her go to her knees. She could only watch helplessly as he undid his pants and stepped out of them, leaving him completely nude.

"God." She drank in the sight of him, from his broad shoulders down to lean hips and lower. Her gaze snagged on a line of black across his ribs, and she ran her fingers over it. "A tattoo?"

"Lord, what fools these mortals be." It was surrounded by an intricate design that had a flavor of the Celtic knot work she'd seen, but somehow managed to be something

else altogether.

"*A Midsummer Night's Dream*? I would think something like *Richard III* is more your style."

"He was just misunderstood." His grin made her knees weak. "Maybe we have that in common."

She hadn't expected to find that he had this softer side, something that might be described as whimsy. Then again, she hadn't expected a lot of things when it came to him. "Maybe you do."

"We can debate Shakespeare later if you'd like. Right now I have other things on my mind." He pushed her panties down, and nudged her to step out of them—and toward the bed. She'd been in his room half a dozen times already, but she'd pointedly ignored this particular piece of furniture every time. There was no ignoring it now. It was massive, and the red bedspread only made it look bigger. The frame was dark wood and simple, but it had an unrelenting masculine vibe that fit Caine perfectly.

He didn't give her a chance to examine it further. She felt him behind her and half expected him to toss her right in the middle of it, but he climbed on and lay on his back. "Come here."

She obeyed almost instantly, following him onto the soft comforter. But when she reached him, she wasn't sure what to do. Climb aboard? Lie next to him? Sit on his face? Addison blushed at the last thought. Where the hell had that come from?

His hands on her hips urged her to straddle him, and the time for thinking passed the second she had his hard length between her legs. Addison kissed him, needing to feel closer, needing to *be* closer. As she moved down his neck, his hand tangled in her hair stopped her. "Tonight is about you, darlin'. Whatever you need, I've got it covered."

She went still, the profound knowledge that he was handing the reins over to her nearly undoing her right then and there. Ever since she met him, he'd been pushing and pulling at her, edging her closer and closer to the point of no return.

And now he was letting her control things?

God, this man made her feel so many things. Things she didn't have a name for, that weren't completely comfortable, but what they boiled down to was that he made her feel alive. Terrifyingly and gloriously alive.

She pressed a kiss to the hollow of his throat. "Okay." Then she resumed her path, working her way down his chest to his stomach and lower.

He went tense, his abs clenching beneath her mouth. "What are you doing?"

"What I want." She grinned against his skin. Even now, even when she was damn near desperate for him, she couldn't help enjoying the way he spoke through clenched teeth when she did something that didn't fit in with his stringent world view. "Isn't that what you just offered?"

He hissed out a breath when she licked his left hip bone. "I'm reconsidering."

"Too late." She slid slower, settling between his legs and taking him in her hand. He started to move, but whatever he was going to do died when she eased his cock between her lips. His muttered curse was music to her ears, but the feel of him in her mouth quickly surpassed that. All that strength, wrapped in smooth skin, and all for her.

His hands tangled in her hair as she worked him, licking

her way down and back up, and then circling his head with her tongue. She was just getting into the rhythm when he cursed again. "Darlin', as much as I'm enjoying this, I'd really like to be inside you this first time."

Well, hell. How was she supposed to argue with that? It was tempting to keep going just to feel him come undone at her hands and mouth, but the truth was that she wanted him inside her this first time, too. She reluctantly released him and sat up. Caine didn't waste any time hauling her back on top of him. He pulled a condom out of the nightstand, but she grabbed it out of his hands.

"Let me." She ripped it open and slowly rolled it over him, the feeling of him in her hands making her entire body shake. She was really doing this, and with Caine. As soon as he was covered, he sat up, nearly unseating her, and kissed her.

"I've wanted this ever since you barged into my office. Maybe before then."

"Before?"

"I saw you at my brother's wedding and everything paled in comparison. Did you know you light up a room when you smile?"

She didn't know what to do with this new side of Caine. He was easy to put into a box when he was growling at her and stomping around with a forbidding expression on his face. But the wicked sense of humor and the way he was looking at her now, as if she were about to give him a gift beyond price? That was something else altogether.

"I've wanted this, too." Even if she hadn't been able to admit it to herself—was *still* having difficulty admitting it to herself.

"Then take it, darlin'. Take *me*."

She'd never taken anyone before. Not like he meant. The power that rose at his words gave her the courage to lift herself onto her knees and sink down, sheathing him in one smooth movement. They froze, their eyes level for the first time that she could remember. His gray gaze held something soft that scared the shit out of her, but she was too caught up with how wonderful it felt to have him inside her to stop. She rocked her hips, taking him a little deeper, the movement rubbing her front along his, sending sparks flying beneath her skin. "That feels good."

"Yeah." His voice was a little strangled, but his hands on her hips urged her on, helping her find the right rhythm to have pressure building deep inside her. She clutched his shoulders and let her eyes slide shut, luxuriating in the feeling of being so close to him. Who knew that a man so tightly wound would be the one to set her free?

Her orgasm hit her, sucking her under like a riptide and sending her hurtling into oblivion. "*Caine.*"

"That's right, darlin', I've got you. I always will."

Chapter Eleven

Caine tried to relearn how to breathe while his world broke apart and realigned itself. He'd known he wanted Addison around more, but he hadn't really thought about what that might mean. The sex had only cemented it. She brought something to his life that he'd never experienced before, and he was going to move heaven and earth to convince her to stay. Permanently.

He stroked a hand down her side. She smiled without opening her eyes, looking relaxed for the first time since he'd met her. "You're beautiful."

"And you're being charming because you just got laid." She caught his hand and brought it to her lips. The sweetness of the gesture charmed him even more than the sex had. Because *this* was what he'd been searching for—someone to share his house with, to make it into an actual home. Exactly like she'd done from the moment she moved in.

"I'm always charming."

"Whatever you have to tell yourself." She smiled and it struck him that she had freckles. How had he never noticed that? He shifted down her body and she lifted her head. "What are you doing?"

"Counting."

She frowned. "Counting?"

"Yeah." He touched the one on her collarbone. "One." Then a small cluster on her chest. "Two, three, four, five."

"Stop it!" She slapped his wrist.

"Six, seven." He moved to her hip. "Eight. Nine."

"Oh my God." She flopped back to the bed. "This is humiliating."

"I disagree." He kissed her thigh. "Ten."

"What happened to my being in charge?"

"That was then. Eleven." He kissed her other thigh. "This is now. Twelve. Thirteen." He moved higher, licking the spot where thigh met hip. "Oh look—"

A howling echoed through the house. Caine glared at the door. "That damn dog is a nuisance."

"Something's wrong. She wouldn't freak out over nothing." Addison wiggled out of his grip and grabbed his dress shirt. Before he got his boxers on, she had the damn thing mostly buttoned up and her panties back in place. He wanted to enjoy the view of her in his shirt, her pale skin wonderfully contrasted with the dark blue fabric, but she was already out the door and gone. He cursed and yanked on his pants. If there *was* something wrong, the idiot woman was rushing headlong into trouble.

He heard her talking and picked up his pace, hurrying down the stairs, and broke into a run when a male voice spoke, too. He skidded around the corner and nearly hit the wall. When he saw the scene in the formal living room, he kind of wished he had. He scrubbed his hand over his face, but it didn't change.

There was his father on the floor, pinned in place by the giant mop dog, with four puppies in his face, yipping. And there was a half-naked Addison, trying to reason with the dog. Caine took a deep breath and marched into the room. "Dad, I'm sorry."

Addison whipped around so fast, she almost fell. "Did you just say *dad*?"

"Get this beast off me this instant."

She spun back around. "I'm so sorry! Gollum, get off of him. This is your grandpa, not a bad man." Gollum didn't look too impressed, but when Addison snagged her collar, she let herself be urged off her prey. Caine didn't think he'd seen his old man quite so out of sorts in his entire life. His father struggled to his feet, his black suit rumpled beyond repair. He glared at Addison, but she was too busy ushering the parade of dogs out the back door to notice.

When he turned that look on Caine, he knew he was in trouble. "What's going on here?"

A thousand excuses and plausible reasons for this tripped over themselves to get out of his throat. It had been like this ever since he could remember. His father would pin him with one of *those* looks, and he'd do whatever it took to make things right, no matter who was at fault. It had gotten to the point where all he did was make his father happy, no matter the cost. It's how he had ended up in the position he was now, CEO of McNeill Enterprises. He didn't necessarily regret that decision, but it was hard to love it when he hadn't really had a choice.

His father looked at Addison again. "Who is that?"

Before he could think up a good response to that—telling his father that she was his matchmaker would just open up a can of worms he wasn't ready to deal with—she smiled and offered her hand. "I'm Addison St. Claire. It's a pleasure to meet you." Trust her to handle the situation as if his father hadn't just basically caught them in bed together.

He looked at her outstretched hand like it was covered in muck, but he had too much of the South in him to ignore the courtesy of a handshake. He let go as soon as politely possible, and Caine didn't miss the way he wiped his hand on his pants. Christ. He stepped between them before his father said something unforgivable. "What can I help you with, Dad?"

"Your secretary said you were on a date." He didn't quite peer around Caine, but he looked like he wanted to. "I thought for sure you'd be home by now. I didn't expect you to have *company*." The way he said it made it sound like she was a two-bit hooker.

He had to get him out of here—the sooner the better. "Why were you looking for me so late?"

"It's not late. *I* was still in the office."

And their mother was no doubt entertaining her lady friends, or engaged in some sort of nonprofit party planning. She wouldn't miss him during his late evenings—she'd stopped throwing a fit about it somewhere around the time Caine turned ten, and started throwing herself into her own activities.

His parents' relationship—or lack of one—was the main reason he hadn't been too keen to settle down anytime soon. Sustaining a marriage when he worked the hours he currently did was impossible. Either the woman would end up hating him, or she'd become a stranger like his mother had.

But now, standing here facing the clear disparity between his father and himself, he had to wonder. There must be a better way, one that didn't involve isolating the people he was supposed to care the most about. His father hadn't made a single sports game or extracurricular activity from the time he was in grade school until he graduated from college. He'd always been working, to the point where Caine never expected him to show up, even if *he* made sure to be there for every varsity football game Brock played in high school. His little brother had deserved more than that, but that was all Caine was capable of giving him.

Was he willing to miss out on his own kid growing up?

Addison's hand on the small of his back snapped him out of it. Whatever the future held, it wasn't going to be decided tonight. First, he had to deal with his old man. "Is there a problem?"

"Gloucester is threatening to pull out of the Richards account."

Why the fuck hadn't he led with that piece of information? "What? They're set to break ground in a few months. They can't back out now." If they did, it'd be disastrous. It'd set them back God knew how long, and cost him an arm and a leg.

"Maybe if you were in your office when Richards called, you'd have found a way to head this off before it became such an issue."

Damn it, but his father was right. He had to fix this. Now. He turned to Addison. "I've got to take care of this."

She smiled, looking for all the world like she actually understood. "Go. I have plenty to occupy myself." She headed for the hallway leading to the room she'd taken over as her own sometime in the past week. His father started to speak—no doubt to lay into him again—but he held up a hand. "I'll take care of it."

By the time Caine caught up with her, she was already in the room and opening her computer. "Hey."

She raised her eyebrows. "That was a quick fix."

"Not quite." He pulled her to her feet. "I wasn't about to leave without my good-bye kiss."

Her eyebrows inched higher. "Good-bye kiss."

"Yeah. It's in the contract."

"I don't remember signing a contract."

"I'll have Agnes email you a copy." He grinned. Even thirty seconds in her presence was enough to loosen the stress threatening to pull him under. He still had to deal with it, but it would be easier to do knowing that she was here, waiting for him.

"You do that. I'd like to know what I signed on for."

Everything. He hauled that word back by the skin of his teeth and kissed her instead. They hadn't even had a chance to talk, so his telling her that he had no intention of letting her go would only scare her. And a scared Addison would fly half of New York's eligible women down here to date him. It wouldn't change a damn thing, but he didn't feel like jumping through hoops that could easily be avoided.

Knowing his father was in the next room kept him from following through on the way she melted against him. Not to mention he had one of his biggest contracts this year threatening to fall through. He refused to let that happen.

The Richards account would bring nearly two hundred jobs into an area of Manchester that desperately needed it. Plus, it was the first project in years that didn't involve him traveling the South to put things together, since it was being built in his hometown.

He pressed a kiss to Addison's forehead. "I wish I could say don't wait up, but it might end up being a late night if my old man isn't exaggerating."

"Like I said, I have work I've been neglecting since I got down here. Take care of your business and I'll be here when you're done."

Did she have any idea what those words did to him? He searched her face, but she seemed genuinely earnest. Like she had no idea she was offering him the world. He kissed her again. "I'll call you later."

"Go, before your father comes in here looking for you and Gollum takes offense again."

With a laugh, he went.

· · ·

Addison set to work on her computer. First, she pulled up all the profiles she'd spent the last week ignoring. It had been months since she wanted to match people with their soul mates. Now it was all she could think about. There were clients who needed to find their love and she was just the person to help them. She smiled as she remembered the look on Caine's face before he left. He really was something. Things with his father hadn't gone particularly well, but there was plenty of time to fix that before she left.

She frowned. Did she still want to leave? Things that

looked so simple before suddenly weren't simple at all. It seemed cliché to say that the sex changed things. But it did. With her body still tingling from his touch, how was she supposed to be thinking about leaving? She frowned harder. Caine wasn't hers. It didn't matter how much she enjoyed him, it couldn't happen. Knowing that shouldn't hurt quite so much, but it did.

Needing a distraction from the trap her mind had become, she opened up her client files. She might be a hot mess in her personal life right now, but she could at least help out people she was working for. Addison got to work bringing up different files and looking at them all at once.

It was something she'd done ever since she started her matchmaking business, to be able to see all clients at once and see if anything stuck out. It didn't always work, but sometimes two people would jump out at her and that would result in a spark on their first date. It was that first spark that had made her love this business initially, but that love had waned over the years. Who knew it would take a grouchy CEO to snap her out of it?

She didn't know if she should be thanking or cursing Caine for twisting her up as much as he had. Either way, it wasn't going to help her tonight. She stared at her computer screen until the faces blurred, but all she could think about was the look in his eyes when he'd pushed into her. There was more than lust there, more than just desire in the damn near reverent way he touched her.

And she'd responded. God, had she responded.

She wasn't getting any work done tonight, no matter how good her intentions were. With a sigh, she shut down the computer and opened the back door. "Gollum! Leo,

Don, Raph, Mikey! Time to come in." She smiled as they obediently trotted in, a little parade of white. Gollum immediately herded the pups into the giant bed Addison bought them the other day, and then settled in. "Good night. Sleep tight."

She climbed the stairs, her mind wandering. It was only when she got to the top that she realized she had no idea where she was supposed to sleep. Would it be too presumptuous to go to his bedroom? Or would she be sending the wrong signal if he came home and she was in her own? She stood there, frozen in place, until Gollum came up and nudged her hip. This was silly. Caine probably wouldn't be home until morning, if then, and she was exhausted. What she needed was sleep—not to be sitting here obsessing about hurting his feelings. If she had half a brain, she'd get on a plane and never look back. But Addison couldn't make herself leave.

She didn't even want to try.

Chapter Twelve

Caine didn't get home until late the next morning. He was pretty sure he had sand in his eyeballs, and his entire body felt as if he'd just run a marathon. But it was worth it because he'd talked Gloucester out of backing out of the deal. Apparently the man had been feeling neglected because Caine was focused on other things. Gloucester was more high-maintenance than any woman he'd met, and he was certainly more high-maintenance than Addison.

Thinking of her brought a smile to Caine's face. Ending the night with another lovemaking session instead of his being called off to work would have been more preferable by far. Once definitely wasn't enough.

He smiled as he pulled into his driveway. Before this week, after a long night, he would have spent a few hours on his couch at his office. Now? Now he couldn't wait to get home. It was more than sex—though the sex was pretty fantastic. Addison brought something to his life that he hadn't even been aware he was missing. Looking back, everything was stark. He'd been so damn miserable, and it was only her busting through the wall he'd built around himself that allowed him to see it.

He never knew what he'd find when he walked through the front door, and damn it, he enjoyed that. Had she taken pity on some other animal and adopted it? She could say that Gollum was to improve his image all she wanted, but that only required one dog. Addison had adopted an entire family because she couldn't bear the thought of a mother being separated from her pups.

Her fierce protectiveness was just one of the many things he found himself drawn to. He had a feeling he'd find even more the longer they spent together.

Christ, he needed sleep. It wasn't like him to sit here and wax poetic about anyone, even a woman as interesting and engaging as this one. But a lot of his personal rules had changed since Addison came into his life. It was enough to make him wonder what else would change if he convinced her to stay.

He half expected her to be in the room she'd taken over as her own, but she was nowhere be found. The dog, however, was all too happy to see him. He let her and her puppies into the backyard, and then set out to find Addison. It was late morning, so he'd expected her to be up. He'd never been so happy to be wrong.

He found her in his room. Caine stopped just inside the door, a feeling he couldn't describe welling up in his chest. She slept in *his* bed last night. What was it about this woman to make him feel so possessive and out of control? He wanted an answer, but at the same time, he wanted to spend the rest of his life figuring it out.

Rest of his life? That was a hell of a long time to spend with someone he had known only a week. Surely he couldn't actually be thinking about forever with her?

And yet…he was.

He stripped off his shirt, taking his time. The sight before him was something to be enjoyed — not rushed. She was exquisite, all that pale skin against his dark red sheets, the tumble of her hair nearly the same color. He made quick work of his pants, and then climbed into bed with her. She rolled toward him but didn't wake up as he settled next to her. If *this* was something he could expect to find in his bed on a regular basis, he might be willing to reconsider his reluctance to settle down permanently. He brushed her hair from her face, tracing her cheekbone with his thumb.

She smiled without opening her eyes. "You're home."

"I'm sorry it took so long."

"You don't have to apologize. I know all about business emergencies." She opened her eyes. "The stories I can tell you would curl your hair. You think working with contractors is bad? Try working with a pair of people who are so determined not to like each other that they actively sabotage a date."

"Sabotage a date? I don't know a damn thing about that." He grinned and pulled her into his arms. "I was in the process of doing something delightful when we were interrupted last night. Let's get back to that."

"Don't you need to sleep?"

"I can sleep when I'm dead. And unless you have plans you're not telling me about, I'm safe for the moment." He rolled on top of her, pinning her wrists above her head. She sighed like this was a serious chore, but the smile tugging at the edges of her mouth told him just how much she was enjoying this. That and the way she leaned up for a kiss. He lost himself in the feeling of her mouth yielding to his, her body soft beneath him, the little tremors in her muscles telling him better than words she was just as affected by this as he was.

Don't leave. He fought the words back. If he wanted Addison to stay, he had to give her a reason. A woman like her wasn't going to be permanently swayed by sex, no matter how hot the chemistry sparked between them.

But it was a start.

He kissed his way down her collarbone, resuming the path he'd taken last night. Her skin was soft beneath his mouth, her body shivering with each lick. He moved over her ribs, spanning her waist with his hands. She was a tiny little thing, something that was easy to forget when she was filling the room with her presence. She offered so many contradictions, and those only seemed to become more pronounced the more time he spent with her.

He spread her thighs and settled between them. "Thinking about this was all that got me through the night. The entire time Gloucester was making his demands, I was thinking about touching you here."

"That's terrible!"

"What do you expect? I was interrupted before I could taste you again last night." He kissed the spot where thigh met hip, loving the way she shuddered. If he'd ever been with a more responsive woman, he couldn't remember one. Hell, every other sexual experience he'd had to date paled in comparison to this. This was special. Unique. Something worth fighting for.

Before she could say anything else, he gave her center a long lick. She tasted better than he remembered. There were too many things he couldn't say yet, so he pushed away everything but her hands in his hair as he drove her wild. He could spend all day drawing those little sounds from her mouth. Each one reminded him that *he* was the only man she'd been with in years.

If he had his way, he'd be the only one she'd be with for years to come.

Her shaking body gave away how close she was to the edge. It wouldn't take much to push her over. He slid a single finger into her and crooked it, making her nearly come off the bed. She lifted her hips, her breath sobbing out as she offered him more. He couldn't have said no if he wanted to. He was starting to think he could deny this woman nothing.

Caine draped her legs over his shoulders, the move spreading her wider for him. He gentled his touch to the lightest of licks over her clit. She whimpered, trying to arch into him, but he wasn't about to let her take control. This time he was in the driver's seat.

"I want to be inside you...feel you coming around my cock."

Her entire body spasmed at his words. "Yes, please, I want that, too."

Needing to do just that, he moved back up her body and blindly reached for the condoms in the top drawer. Addison kissed him as he rolled one on, her body arching up to meet his. He slid into her slowly, relishing the connection. Caine pumped once, twice, gauging her reactions. When one angle made her go wild beneath him, he propped himself on his elbows and worked at re-creating it.

Her head thrashed from side to side. "God, that feels so good."

It did. Too damn good. He gritted his teeth, determined to drive her out of her mind before he let go. Her fingers dug into his ass and she kissed him with a desperation that matched his own. Then she was coming, her core milking him until he couldn't stop himself from driving into her, chasing the pressure building in the small of his back. His orgasm hit him like a freight train, and he groaned her name as he came.

He slid to the side and kissed her one last time. "The things you do to me."

"God, you're insatiable." She smiled. "But you need to get some sleep. You've been up all night."

"Just a few hours. I have to check in again with Gloucester this afternoon to ensure nothing else goes wrong." As happy as he'd be to spend the entire day with her in bed, he was after more. Which meant it was time to implement the *more.* "Why don't you let me take you out this evening?"

"Out?"

"Yes." He paused, wondering why this felt so incredibly important after everything they'd experienced in the last twenty-four hours. "On a date."

She flinched, just a little, but managed to dredge up a smile. "That'd be wonderful."

Funny, but normally when he asked out a woman he knew for a fact was interested in him—something he couldn't misinterpret when it came to Addison—she didn't cringe. "I promise not to bite."

"I bet you say that to all the ladies." She scooted out from beneath his arm. "Get some sleep. I still have work to do if I'm going to be jaunting about with you tonight."

There was something off about her response, but she kissed him and walked out of the room before he could pinpoint the issue. Caine debated chasing her down and figuring out what the problem was—and doing whatever necessary to ensure she didn't fly in another woman while he slept—but exhaustion tugged at him. If she wasn't in the sharing mood right now, which her quick exit seemed to indicate, she wasn't going to appreciate him chasing her down and demanding to talk. He'd get some sleep and allow her a chance to find her footing again before tonight.

Tonight she wouldn't have the opportunity to run from him when he asked her what was wrong.

• • •

Addison managed to spend the rest of the day very carefully not thinking. She was getting pretty good at it. There was a healthy dose of panic sitting at the back of her mind, patiently waiting for her to let her guard down, but she refused to give in. No matter how uncertain the future felt right now, she truly was enjoying her time with Caine. Everything else would work itself out in the end, and it would most definitely *not* blow up in her face.

Maybe if she told herself that enough times, she'd actually start to believe it.

She took extra time to shower, letting hot water beat some stress from her tired muscles. As expected, this house had excellent water pressure. Everything about this place was excellent. Hell, everything about Caine was excellent, too. What was a mere mortal like her supposed to do in the face of all that personality and drive? She hadn't stood a chance.

She still didn't.

She washed her hair with the flowery-smelling shampoo, and couldn't help wondering if it belonged to a woman who had been here before. She didn't like to think she'd been wrong about his lack of social life, though she could admit to herself that the reasons *why* it bothered her weren't professional ones. She was up to her neck and sinking fast when it came to the man. When she'd met him that first day, she hadn't expected to be so wrong about him. He might be as miserable as she'd thought—it took one to know one—but there was so much more going on beneath his gruff exterior. The thread of unexpected tenderness was what really got her. Every time he touched her, it was as if he was holding the most breakable thing in the universe and he didn't want to hurt her.

Which just went to show—he saw and understood a lot more about her than was entirely comfortable.

She dried off and headed to the closet. As she always did the rare times she traveled, she had unpacked as soon as she got here. What seemed like a lot of clothes before now felt like not nearly enough. What does one wear on a date with the millionaire, especially one she *liked*? Surely not the same thing she'd worn to the interview? She didn't know.

But she knew someone who would.

Addison picked up her phone and dialed the number from memory. As expected, Reagan picked up quickly. "Hello, sweetie."

She sounded entirely too chipper. Addison frowned. Reagan couldn't have known what would happen when she sent her down here. That was too diabolical, even for her friend. Except… She pushed the worry from her mind. Right now she had bigger fish to fry. "I don't know what to wear on a date."

There was a long pause. "A date?"

"…Yes."

An even longer pause. "And who might this date be with?"

Did she admit it? Normally Regan wouldn't be judgmental about such things, but Addison's instincts had been wrong from the beginning when it came to Caine. Maybe she was wrong about this too. She cursed herself. Why would she have called if she didn't trust Regan? Now was not the time to doubt herself. "Caine."

Her friend didn't miss a beat. "What have you got with you?"

She breathed a sigh of relief. She should have known Regan wouldn't interrogate her when there was a fashion emergency on the line. "A bunch of professional dresses."

"That's not going to work."

Which was exactly the problem. "Yeah, I know. Hence the panicked phone call to you."

"I'm trying not to enjoy this too much." She laughed. "But I never thought I'd see the day—Addison going on a date."

"Please don't blow this out of proportion. It's just one date." Even speaking that aloud felt like a lie. This *was* a big deal, whether she liked it or not.

"And when was your last date?"

Regan already knew this. She was the only one other than Grandmother that Addison had told about Lee, though she'd taken a very different approach. "Six years ago," she mumbled.

"So, my point stands. This is a big deal. What time are you going out?"

She hadn't actually asked. She'd been too worried about getting out of Caine's bed before she gave in to the temptation to touch him again—and before he followed through on the look he'd given her when she left the room. The one that said he knew something was wrong and he had no intention of letting it go. "I'm not sure."

"Typical man. But I bet he's more punctual than his brother."

Easy to be punctual when he hadn't pinpointed a time. God, that wasn't fair. She hadn't exactly given him an opportunity to settle the details. Thank goodness she'd called Regan, because she was in danger of spiraling into psychosis before the date itself rolled around. "I don't know what to do."

"I have a simple solution. Go shopping."

"Regan! I can't just drop everything and go shopping."

"And what exactly is more important than your first date in six years?"

Addison glared at her computer. There were nearly a dozen emails demanding her attention, but she couldn't say as much to Regan. The woman would undoubtedly point out that if they were vitally important, someone would have called instead of emailed. "Work."

"Work can wait. Dates cannot."

She killed a protest before it got past her lips. Wasn't this exactly the excuse she'd been looking for when she called? It was pathetic that she apparently needed permission to go shopping, but nothing about this situation was her norm. "You know, maybe you're right."

"Sweetie, I always am."

And wasn't that the truth? Regan was known for her ability to read people. Besides, she wanted to buy a new dress, so she was going to buy a new dress. Something to really knock his socks off. "You shouldn't let it go to your head."

"Too late." She laughed. "Buy something in white or green. You look amazing in them both."

"Thank you."

"What are friends for if not giving you an excuse to go shopping? I expect a call with full details tomorrow. Now have fun." She hung up, leaving Addison feeling much better about the whole thing, with the added bonus that shopping would keep her mind off all the reasons going on a date with Caine was a terrible idea.

She just had to hang on to that confidence through the date. Easy as pie.

Too bad she didn't believe it.

Chapter Thirteen

Caine slept later than intended, but if anything, the extra hour gave him more energy at the office. Gloucester was still on board, and no new problems had arisen in the last twelve hours. He'd even managed to make it home by five — the first time in as long as he could remember. But then, a lot of his life was different these days.

He bounded up the stairs and into his room, almost disappointed when he found it empty. Surely she hadn't taken off? He almost laughed at the irrational thought. There was nothing wrong beyond her being uncomfortable because he was pushing her boundaries a little. There was nothing horrifically wrong. In fact, things were more right than they had ever been. He had a woman in his life who challenged him in a way he never thought possible, and this old house actually felt like a home for the first time since he was in grade school. Things were working out perfectly. He just had to enjoy his time with Addison and stop overthinking things.

He showered quickly, his mind already on the upcoming date. He already knew where he was taking Addison — a little hole-in-the-wall bar and grill he frequented. She'd seen the element of his life that came with having money, and she was less than impressed with it. Rightfully so. He'd been born to money. Yes, he'd done well for his family's company, but he couldn't claim he was doing anything other than toeing the line. A glamorous restaurant where everything cost a fortune wasn't going to impress her. Her lack of care when it came to his finances was one of the growing list of things he liked about her.

So he'd show her what had become his hideaway over the years. It was the one place where he was always left alone and no one expected anything of him. In there he wasn't Caine McNeill, CEO of McNeill Enterprises. He was just a man, enjoying a drink.

He couldn't help wondering if she would understand the significance of him taking her there.

He dressed in his favorite pair of slacks, choosing a deep green shirt because he thought she'd like it. At least it wasn't gray. He smiled at the thought. He seemed to be doing that a lot lately — smiling for no reason. If he wasn't careful, he was going to get a reputation.

Once he'd thrown on some cologne, he went in search of Addison. He looked in the room she had taken as hers, but found it empty. Next he moved down to the formal sitting room she had taken as her office, but that was empty as well. Before he had a chance to wonder if his paranoid thoughts weren't, in fact, that paranoid, he caught the faint strains of music coming from somewhere deeper in the house. Caine followed the sound, passing through rooms he hadn't seen in ages.

It struck him that the only place here where he spent any time was in his bedroom. He had a staff whose job it was to keep the rest clean, but he had no reason to wander elsewhere. The endlessly empty rooms always made him feel so lonely. This gigantic house was meant to be filled with laughter and the patter of little feet. Even though it was decorated tastefully enough for even the snobbiest dinner party guests, every piece of furniture was built to last.

If it could survive him and Brock growing up, both rowdy boys with more energy than sense, then it could survive anything. He stopped in the doorway to one of the many living rooms, smiling at the memory of them pretending the floor was lava and jumping from one couch to the next.

The smile died at the memory of their father's reaction. It was one of the rare trips home during the day and he'd been furious to see them "disrespecting" their home. The man never had time for them until they hit junior high, and then all he cared about was ensuring that the McNeill family legacy was carried on.

Caine suspected it was the only reason he'd had children in the first place. It certainly wasn't to love and care about them. He shook his head and moved on. His familial issues aside, this place had been empty too long. With only him living there, it was all too easy to believe in some of the ghost stories the locals told.

He found Addison in one of the many rooms that had been used for entertaining. Caine stopped just inside the door, drinking in the sight of her playing piano. Her fingers danced over keys, graceful despite the fact that she had her eyes closed. He couldn't place the piece she played—something beautiful and haunting that teased him, recognition just out of reach.

He waited, content to let her finish. There hadn't been many peaceful moments in the last week, and he was happy to enjoy this one without interruption. The music spiraled up and up, telling a story of love and loss. It tugged something in his chest, making him wonder why she chose this particular piece—whom she was thinking about when she played it. He leaned against the wall and crossed his arms over his chest. He was overthinking things again. It hadn't been a problem he possessed before meeting this particular woman.

She finished with one last long sad note and opened her eyes. "Hey there." She didn't seem surprised to see him standing there, so she must have heard him coming. He found that he liked the fact that she'd kept playing even though she'd gained an audience.

"That was beautiful. Beethoven?"

She laughed. "'Say Something' by A Great Big World. It hasn't been around long, but every time I hear it, it hits me in the chest. It's so sad and bittersweet."

The question rose again. Whom did she think about when she played that song? Was it her dead husband? Another man somewhere in her past? If she'd gone without for six years, that meant there had been someone else along the way. He couldn't bring himself to ask. Caine had learned a long time ago not to ask questions he didn't want the answers to. This one sure as fuck qualified. "I didn't know you played."

"It's not something I do often. But nothing takes you away quite like music."

"Do you get extra points for playing it yourself?"

"It depends on who you ask." She closed the lid. "Do you play?"

"No." He walked over and ran his hand over the polished surface. "My mother used to, but she hasn't touched this thing in decades." She'd stopped playing right around the time she started up with her nonprofits. "Instruments aren't something I ever tried."

"I'm sure you have more than your fair share of skills." She stood, and he forgot how to breathe. The loose green dress should have looked like a tent with the way it hung off her frame, but instead the cutouts from her shoulders to wrists drew the eye, and the way it billowed around her thighs made him wonder what she was wearing underneath. The damn thing was more tempting than any little black dress he'd ever seen.

She raised a single eyebrow. "You're staring."

"You've been dressed to kill every time I've seen you, but this is above and beyond." He shook his head. "You look amazing. Better than amazing. I'm actually looking for a word to describe it and coming up short."

"For someone supposedly speechless, you sure are saying a lot."

"You have that effect on me." Now that he could finally tear his eyes away from the dress, he took in the rest of the image she presented. Her long red hair was coiled on top of her head, drawing his attention to her long neck, which led him down to the dress again. He put some serious consideration into skipping dinner and taking her up to his bed so he could find out exactly what lay beneath it.

Goddamn it, no. If he wanted Addison to take him seriously, he had to seduce her mind the same way he'd seduced her body.

That started with taking her out on a date.

While he'd been lost in thought, she'd been doing an examination of her own. "Green looks good on you."

"Better than gray?"

She laughed. "Much better."

"Are you going to accuse me of showing off my money if we take the Jaguar tonight?" It was still warm enough to put the top down, and he wanted her to experience the intoxicating beauty that was a Tennessee night. His motivation was transparent, even to himself, but he wasn't about to change his plans.

"I make no promises." Her heels clicked on the wood floor. They weren't particularly tall, but the straps crisscrossing her ankles made her legs look even longer. Christ, he'd be lucky if he made it through dinner without hauling her into the nearest bathroom.

She slipped her hand into the crook of his arm. It was such an innocent touch compared to how intimate they'd been that morning, but it made something clunk in his chest that wasn't entirely comfortable. He wanted her in a way that had little to do with the need pulsing beneath his skin. The fact that she played piano fascinated him. Since his mother had played, it was something he'd contemplated pursuing when he was a kid. His old man had nixed that as soon as he'd asked. There was no time for him to pursue such silly distractions when he was being groomed to take over the company.

What other skills did Addison have?

The question was easier to follow than poking at the aching in his chest that seemed to crop up whenever he was around her, so he focused on that. Safer.

Yes, if he could just stay focused on safer things, there was nothing at all to worry about.

. . .

Addison might disapprove of the Jaguar on principle, but even she couldn't deny the delights of feeling the wind on her face and the warmth of the fall evening on her skin. It was like driving through a different world down here—one from another, simpler time. There hadn't been another car in sight in twenty minutes, and the night seemed larger than life. They might as well be on their own planet, taking the twisting road through the trees. She missed the tall buildings and constant sound of New York City, but this place was downright magical.

Kind of like Caine.

She shot a look sideways, warm all over again at the sight of him handling the sports car with ease. "Take it faster."

He grinned and did as she asked, opening the engine up and sending them hurtling into the night. Addison closed her eyes and tilted her head back, freeing the giddy laugh bubbling up inside her. It was so difficult to hold on to her concerns about the future and him with the wind carrying the scent of some flower she couldn't identify and the moon large in the sky. All she wanted to do was live in the moment and let go of all the things troubling her.

Worry had no place here.

All too soon, he slowed the car and guided them toward town. With every trip to Nashville, she loved it a little more. It was so different from back home, the flavor of the city like something out of a story. Rationally, she knew it had its negatives just like anywhere else, but it didn't stop her from smiling every time she drove through.

Though she expected him to turn toward the restaurant where he'd taken his other dates, Caine headed toward a different part of town, one she'd never been to before. It was quieter here, somewhere she could easily picture men and women strolling beneath the trees lining the street.

He parked on the street, then walked around the car to open her door. The feeling of his hand on the small of her back sent a quiet thrill through her body. It was amazing how much he could affect her with one tiny touch. And the way he had looked at her in the music room? Desire flared just thinking about it. He looked like he wanted to bend her over the bench and take her right there.

She would have loved every second of it.

She never thought she'd be into sex that was so overwhelming and desperate, but after that night on the dining room table she started eyeing his furniture in a whole new way. Would he take her on the couch in the formal living room? Or how about the kitchen counter? Maybe his wonderful shower with no less than *three* showerheads? It made her hot all over just thinking about it.

She was thankful the night darkening the streets hid the blush she could feel staining her cheeks. This wasn't like her at all. She'd certainly enjoyed making love before now, but it had never swept her away on this level. It seemed like every other waking moment was spent either remembering what Caine had done to her body or imagining what else he might do. He made her more hormonal and lusty than a teenager.

The restaurant was not like anything she expected. Instead

of high-class and expensive style, this place was almost a dive bar. There was a scattering of beat-up tables around the room, and even more beat-up stools at the bar. The bartender himself looked like he would have been at home in an old Western, with his faded flannel shirt, a truly impressive beard, and a cowboy hat pulled down low on his head.

She glanced at Caine, wondering if this was joke. But he smiled at the bartender. "Hey JR, how are things?"

"Same as always. Haven't seen your pretty face darkening our door in quite some time."

Caine towed her toward the bar, peanut shells crunching under her heels. "Been busy. Lots of work, and people trying to make my life more complicated."

"Who is this pretty young thing you have with you?"

He slipped an arm around her waist. "JR, I'd like you to meet Addison. She's an honest-to-God matchmaker."

The bartender suddenly seemed to take more interest in her. He tilted his cowboy hat back and eyed her with shockingly pale blue eyes. "A matchmaker, eh? Now that's something you don't see everyday."

"Thank God for that." Caine laughed. "Can we get two shots of whiskey, and two beers?"

"Sure thing."

Addison waited until they took their seat at the end of the bar before she spoke. "I don't drink beer."

"Darlin', you've been turning my life upside down ever since we met. Now it's my turn to expand your horizons." He winked and nudged her with his knee. "Come on, live a little."

Wasn't that what she'd been doing since the beginning? She'd gone and thrown away every single one of her rules for him. Changing up her beverage choices shouldn't seem like that big a deal in comparison. But it did. She took a deep breath and tried to get a hold of her irritation, but the slow exhale did nothing. Her life had been spiraling out of control ever since she agreed to fly down here to take a look at Brock's brother. Having to drink beer was just the icing on the cake.

But then Caine squeezed her thigh, a bare inch below the hem of her dress, effectively reminding her that she wasn't wearing a whole lot beneath it. It wouldn't take much for him to find out how little—just a couple inches higher and he'd find her completely bare. The possibility of him exploring her with his fingers drowned out her growing anger better than any Valium.

"Are you going to tell me what's been bothering you since this morning?"

He'd noticed? She'd thought she had a handle on things, had stuffed them down enough that no one would notice, but apparently she couldn't even do that right. It wasn't as if she could tell him that she was bothered by just how much she liked him. Caine wouldn't understand. He lived in a world where black was black and white was white. To him the fact that they had an obvious attraction between them wasn't an issue—it was something to be pursued.

He didn't even believe in soul mates.

Needing the focus off her before they ended up fighting about that again, Addison changed the subject. "I'm surprised you frequent a place like this enough to be on a first-name basis with the bartender." It was a stay of execution more than anything else—they would have to talk about it eventually. But she wanted to have this night of happiness before reality intruded.

Caine frowned, and for a moment, she was sure he'd pursue his earlier line of questioning, but then he seemed to decide to let go. "It used to be that Brock never met a drinking establishment that he wouldn't frequent. This was one of his favorites when he still lived down here."

She hadn't met his little brother until after he'd moved to New York to be with Regan, but some of the stories he told gave the impression that he'd made a lot of questionable decisions while trying to escape the constant disappointment his father always turned on him. She couldn't imagine what it had been like growing up with that. Both her parents were incredibly supportive of whatever choices she made in life. They might not always agree, but they recognized that she wasn't a little clone of them that had been created solely so that they could have a second chance at life.

It was enough to make her wonder how Caine felt about his father. It wasn't something they'd talked about yet. They'd done an excellent job of avoiding the majority of the deep conversations people who were rapidly falling for each other had.

Addison took a deep breath and let it go. She was supposed to be enjoying the evening—not obsessing about things she wasn't sure she wanted to change. "Brock's not like that these days. He's really settled into being a father." Both he and Regan had taken to parenthood like ducks to water. They showered the twins with love and affection and were even talking about having more children once the girls were potty trained.

And she was happy for them. Really, she was.

But that didn't stop the little spike of envy that went through her every time she held one of the girls. Or spent time with them. Or even thought about them. They seemed to grow by leaps and bounds every time Addison saw pictures of them. It was just another reminder of all the possibilities that had been torn from her along with Aiden.

Caine's squeezing her knee brought her back to herself. "I come here when I want to get away from it all."

"Get away." It sounded like a dream. But she couldn't escape the thoughts in her head as easily as she caught a flight out of New York.

"Yeah. Here, no one expects anything from me except a good tip."

It made a certain amount of sense. As CEO, he was in demand every second of every day—or at least that was how it appeared. In the days she'd been here, the only place other than home that he spent time was the office. No one could live under that level of stress indefinitely without breaking.

How long did he have?

After five years of her company being her life, she felt brittle and so unhappy there were days when every breath hurt. Caine had been CEO for fifteen, and if Brock's comments were anything to go by, he'd worked full-time for McNeill Enterprises even longer. No wonder his misery had been practically radiating from him when they met.

Everyone had to have a place where they felt safe, a place where they could go and let some of the stress of normal life fall away. With people like Addison and Caine, that place was often the only thing that got them through the day.

And he'd brought her to his.

Chapter Fourteen

Caine made a conscious decision to let his concerns about Addison go. Yes, she'd changed the subject when he flat-out asked her what was wrong, but the whole point of tonight was to make her comfortable and show her how good things outside the bedroom could be between them. The rest of the date had gone well, their conversation easy and light and full of laughter. It was only when they were back in the Jaguar that he brought up the idea he'd been mulling over for most of the evening. "I'd like you to meet my parents."

It was hard to tell in the shadows, but he thought her eyes might have gone wide. "Your parents?"

"Yeah."

"Technically, I've already met your father."

Which had been a clusterfuck from beginning to end. His father hadn't had to say anything to get his opinion across. He didn't approve of Addison, but that was because he didn't *know* Addison. There is no way the old man could spend any time in her presence and not be charmed. In order for that to happen, though, he had to get them together in a respectable situation, and for *that* he needed her cooperation. "That hardly counts, and you know it."

She sighed, the sound barely audible over the rush of the wind. "First a date, and now you want me to meet the parents. I don't know what to think of you."

Why did she have to think anything? Because when a woman made comments like that, it didn't mean anything positive. He hadn't dated much in recent years, but he remembered that just fine.

Which brought the point home that she wasn't all right. "I asked you before, and when you changed the subject, I let you. Now I'm going to ask you again, and I want an answer—what's wrong?"

She was quiet so long, he thought she might dodge the question yet again. But then she turned in her seat to face him. "I told you I haven't been with anyone in six years. There's a reason it's been so long."

He knew that, but he wasn't about to confess that he'd been checking up on her. Besides, he wanted to hear what happened directly from Addison. He'd trusted her enough to take her to his bar, and she seemed to understand the significance of that. Now it seemed she was returning the favor of trust. "Tell me."

"When I was in high school, I was the perfect daughter, student, and friend. And I loved it. I loved pleasing other people, and I loved school in general." She looked out the window. "There was a boy—isn't there always?—and as much as I was everything to everyone else, he was everything to me. He was my rock, and he was there for me whenever I needed him. Everyone thought it was just young love, the kind that flares hot and only lasts a moment."

He only knew about that stuff—in theory. Caine had dated in high school, but nothing particularly serious. He'd had friends who fell in love, and some even married their high school sweethearts. But like so many statistics, over the years most of those relationships had ended in divorce.

"We got married the summer after high school, and I was so happy I'm surprised I didn't burst from it."

He wasn't sure what he expected to hear in her voice when she talked about this boy-man she'd loved, but there was nothing but a bittersweet tone. She wasn't seeing Caine anymore, or even the present—her gaze had gone into the past where he couldn't follow. "I had three years with the love of my life—my one true soul mate—before he died, and a decent portion of those were spent apart."

"How did he die?" He already knew, but hearing it from Regan and hearing it straight from Addison felt like two completely different stories happening to two different people.

"He was in the Army. He wanted a job that was going to provide for us while I went to college." She shook her head. "I never went. I kept putting it off because I wanted to be there for him when he wasn't deployed. And after he was gone, I just didn't have the heart for it."

He hated hearing this, hated knowing she thought this dead man was the only one for her. "You seem to have done pretty damn well for yourself."

She shrugged. "It started off innocently enough. I had a group of friends determined to get me out of my house on a semi-regular basis. I saw that two of them would be amazing as a couple, so I pushed one and pulled the other." She smiled for the first time since they'd started talking about this. "They just had their fourth baby and are still madly in love."

There it was—that wistfulness that he'd heard when they spoke at the bar. That wasn't the tone of a woman ready to be done with the possibilities of life. He'd have to be blind to miss the longing in every line of her body. She wanted kids. Maybe it made him a bastard to want to take her out of the corner she'd painted herself into, but he wanted to be the one to give her that dream. A more honorable man would respect her wishes in this and let their affair fizzle out.

Over his dead body.

But he'd figure out how he'd change her mind later. Right now he needed to keep her talking. "And then?"

"And then things just sort of spiraled out of control. I loved watching my friends fall in love. It was the first time I'd felt alive since Aiden died, and so I grabbed on to it with both hands."

Because she wasn't ready to join him in the grave—even figuratively. He wondered if she realized what her actions meant, though all signs seemed to indicate she didn't. "I think it's amazing what you've put together. What's your success rate up to now?"

"I don't choose to measure success in rates or percentages. It takes the heart out of the business to say I have a ninety percent successful match rate. But since I've started my own business, I've been invited to nearly a hundred weddings."

Christ. "Did you make it to all of them?"

She frowned. "Yeah. It's the realization of a happily ever after between two soul mates. It'd be wrong if I didn't go."

The crux of the problem of a potential future with them— she still believed that soul mate crap. Which wasn't to say he *didn't* believe. But limiting yourself to only one person for the entirety of your life was pretty damn shortsighted. Her husband died when she was twenty-one. By her theory, she should spend the rest of her life alone because he was the only one for her. It was bullshit.

He didn't particularly like being jealous of a dead man, but Caine couldn't help himself. "What happens if one of them dies?"

She jerked back as if he'd struck her. "Why would you say something like that?"

"I'm serious. What if one of these married couples was in a car accident and one of them, let's say the wife, dies."

"Caine—"

"Humor me, please."

She bit her lip, looked away, and finally shrugged. "That would be a terrible tragedy."

"I'm not arguing that. But what if, say, five years later, the husband comes to you, looking for you to match him again."

Her gaze flew back to him. "What the hell kind of scenario is this?"

"You're humoring me, remember?" She glared, but he wasn't about to let that deter him. He could argue until he was blue in the face that she was entitled to being happy with someone besides her dead husband and it would change nothing. This was the only way to make her see. Addison was pretty damn protective of her clients. She wouldn't sentence one to a life of loneliness and misery just because she believed each person only got one soul mate per lifetime. "Would you match him?"

"He already had his soul mate."

That wasn't an answer. "But would you match him? This

guy is begging you to help him out. He's tried dating, and I'm sure you know what that shit is like, and he's tried being set up by friends, but nothing's clicked. All he wants is to share his life with someone." And then he went in for the kill. "He wants kids, darlin'. He wants to be a grandfather some day."

"God, *stop*."

He couldn't. Not until he made her see. "Then answer the question. Would you turn him away?"

"*I don't know*. Does it make you happy to know that? I...I don't know." She shifted in her seat, facing the passenger window.

Damn it, that wasn't the answer he'd been after. He wanted her to admit that she'd help that poor guy, which would lead her to the logical conclusion that if she could find happiness for that client, then there was no reason *she* couldn't find happiness again.

Caine gripped the wheel and turned them toward home. He'd planted the seed in her head. He hoped. Other than forcing her to look at the issue from this perspective, he wasn't sure what else he could say to change her mind... but he had damn well better figure it out quickly if he didn't want her to walk out of his life. "Darlin' — "

"I don't want to talk about this anymore. Why can't we keep things simple — have fun and enjoy each other's company?"

He didn't want this to end. He wanted this thing with Addison to be more than just enjoying each other's company. He wanted her to *stay*. But how the hell was Caine supposed to convince her of that if she refused to talk about a potential future at every turn?

They pulled up in front of his house, all the outside lights lit up to welcome them home. *Home*. It was a concept he'd gotten used to since she moved in, and he wasn't keen on letting go. The thought of this giant house becoming empty again was almost more than he could bear. Bad enough that he had the memories from childhood, but to have something so recent—something he hadn't realized he wanted desperately—and then lose it... Caine would do damn near anything to keep that from happening.

He got out of the car, determined to close the chasm that had opened up between them during their conversation. She barely got a foot onto the driveway when he pulled her into his arms. The dress was softer than he'd expected, the fabric so light it was almost nonexistent. Good. He wanted as few barriers between them as possible. Caine smoothed his hand down her back and nothing broke the movement. He went still. "You aren't wearing anything under this, are you?"

Her smile took on a wicked edge. "I was wondering when you'd notice."

"You've been like this all night." He slid his hands beneath the hem of her dress, his concerns over the future falling away at the feel of her body beneath his palms. Fuck. If he'd known she'd left out that particular piece of her wardrobe, good intentions or no, he really wouldn't have made it through dinner.

There was nothing stopping them from doing it now. Keeping one arm around her waist, he maneuvered his free hand between her legs. She opened for him, already tilting her hips in invitation. He pressed his palm to her center and groaned when he found her wet and ready for him.

Caine kissed her as he drew a finger through her wetness. His desperation had been building all night—desperation to make her see that there really was something between them, desperation to know her better, desperation to bury himself deep inside her. He couldn't wait any longer. Still kissing her, he reached around her and popped open the dashboard. There was a God in heaven because condom wrappers crinkled beneath his hand. "I'm going to take you now, darlin'."

"Good."

She had his pants undone by the time he ripped open the condom. He rolled it on, kissing her one more time. From there, it was the easiest thing in the world to pick her up and sink himself deep inside her. That first stroke took him to heaven and back. Her whimpers only magnified the sensation. How could she continue to deny the connection between them? It was so strong he could almost see it.

He spread her wider and shoved in again, driving her back against the car. It was too rough, too crazed, but he couldn't stop, not with her grip urging him on and her moaning in his ear. "Come for me, darlin'. Only me."

"I—"

He cut her off with a kiss, because if she contradicted him right now he wasn't sure he could recover. Knowing that struck a note through him that was damn near panic. She might very well walk away from this, leaving him broken and bloody behind her.

And then he couldn't think anymore because she was coming, her body clenching around him, her heels digging into the small of his back, her hands in his hair. He couldn't hang on any longer so he drove into her, losing himself in the feel of her surrounding him. It was too damn good— better than good. Fucking outstanding.

How the hell was he going to convince her to stay?

Chapter Fifteen

Addison tried—and failed—to focus on work. Her people had been doing just fine without her, but her second-in-command, James, had sent a flurry of emails this morning complaining about Sarah Roberts. Apparently she was on a warpath, demanding to be set up on a date immediately in order to compensate her for the fiasco that was Caine Mc-Neill. If this mess wasn't landing squarely on Addison's lap, she might find the whole thing amusing. While she waited for her curling iron to heat up, she typed a quick email back recommending that James show Sarah the newest bachelor who had signed on two days before Addison left New York. He was an up-and-comer, and he was already making waves on the firewall software scene. Maybe he'd snap Sarah out of her funk. And who knew? They might even be a match.

Stranger things had happened.

Like the fact that Addison was sleeping with Caine, when she was supposed to be matching him with his soul mate. That was pretty damn strange. She knew what he'd been trying to do last night with his pointed questions, but he was wrong.

Each person only got one soul mate—it was the glorious and tragic truth of life.

But then why couldn't she stop thinking about the theoretical man he'd asked her about? It wasn't a situation she'd encountered, so she'd never really thought about it. Oh, there were divorcees on her list, and had been since she started Connected at the Lips. She'd always chalked it up to their marrying the wrong person. People got married for all the wrong reasons all too often—picking the person who wasn't their soul mate just topped out the list.

That wasn't the situation Caine had proposed, though. This man was someone who'd had the love of his life—his soul mate—and lost her.

What would she do? It didn't seem fair to try to match someone when she knew there was no way they could find a second soul mate. Really, it was almost cruel. She would just be setting them up for disappointment.

But could she really turn a person away when doing so seemed to go against everything she stood for?

She shook her head. Thinking about this made her brain hurt, which she suspected Caine knew. He was trying to get her to admit that soul mates didn't exist, but she just couldn't. There was too much evidence to indicate they did. Look at her grandparents, one of the most romantic and, yes, tragic love stories she'd ever encountered. And her parents. After thirty years of marriage that had seen some serious trials along the way, they came out the other side happier than ever.

Plus, she wouldn't be in the business she was in if soul mates didn't exist.

Caine had known exactly how hard to push her, though, because after they had sex against the car last night, he held her hand while they walked inside and then tucked them both into bed.

This whole thing with him had turned sort of…domestic. And it was surprisingly comfortable—*scarily* comfortable might be more accurate description. She and Aiden hadn't really had a chance to settle into any kind of life together. As soon as they graduated from high school, he'd gone and joined the military. It had felt like the right decision at the time, and eventually, she'd even gotten to the point where she stopped resenting the choice they made. To Aiden, there was no greater calling than to serve his country. She'd have hurt him if she'd insisted he do something else.

He wouldn't have died if he'd done something else.

To be sharing these experiences for the first time with Caine instead of the man who was supposed to be her soul mate…

She froze. Supposed to be? Where the hell had that come from? She never once doubted Aiden was her soul mate. She wasn't now. She couldn't be. God, her life had been so much easier before she met Caine and started questioning everything she'd once thought was true. She craved him with a fierceness she didn't know how to combat. Worse, it seemed to only be growing stronger as time went on.

Addison sent her email and silently wished James the best of luck. He was going to need it dealing with Sarah Roberts. The rest of her in-box wasn't vitally important, so she closed her computer. It had been hours since she saw

Caine last and a part of her already missed him. What was he doing right now? Poring over contracts? Arguing with someone on the phone? Would he work through lunch if left to his own devices?

Before she could question the impulse too thoroughly, she changed into a loose shirt and the only pair of jeans she'd brought, slipped on her shoes, and headed out to her car.

Fifteen short minutes later, she was sitting in front of his office building and wondering what the hell she was doing. He was still putting out fires from whatever had gone wrong the other night. Her showing up wasn't going to do anything but waste his time. In addition to that, it would all but explicitly tell him that he and his uncomfortable questions were getting to her.

But she couldn't make herself drive away.

There had to be something she was missing when it came to this thing with him. It was the only explanation for the feelings twisting up inside her, and the only way to figure it out was to spend more time with Caine. Their nights together weren't enough. To be honest, the nights had become part of the problem because the mind-blowing sex was only further muddying the issue.

The only solution was to find a way to spend time with him when he wasn't at home.

Satisfied her reasons were beyond reproach, she got out of her car and headed for the building. A few people smiled at her as she crossed the lobby, but that air of goodwill died when she reached his office. The secretary pushed to her feet as Addison came through the door, her expression forbidding. "He's busy."

"I'm not here to distract him."

The look the woman gave her put to rest any effort at being cordial. Obviously she wasn't going to get anywhere by being polite.

She sighed. "Please tell him I'm here."

"I said—"

"Because if you don't, I'm just going to charge past you and make you look bad again." Knowing he was so close had her heartbeat thundering just beneath her skin. She wanted to see him—needed to see him. "Now, please."

The secretary glared daggers, but she made the call. She looked like she was about to spit nails at whatever Caine said. "Yes, sir." She placed the phone down with a care that suggested what she really wanted to do was throw it across the room. "He'll see you now."

"Thank you." She headed for his office, barely resisting the urge to rotate as she moved so she wouldn't give the woman her back.

She found Caine at his desk, once again buried in paperwork. The smile that stretched across his face was nearly identical to the one he'd sent her from the exact same place the first time she saw him. It hit her that her entire life had altered course starting the moment she walked through this door a little less than a week ago. "Hey."

"Have you already eaten?"

Trust him to recognize how off-center she was and move to put them on even ground by doing away with small talk. She tucked her hair behind her ears. "No, not yet."

"I haven't, either. I'm starving." His tone of voice brought forth the question—was he starving for her, or starving for food?

He didn't move from behind the desk, but his gaze made it feel like he was drinking in the sight of her. She couldn't remember the last man who'd been so openly appreciative of how she looked—or that she'd cared so much what he thought of her.

She licked her lips. "I am, too."

"Do you want to go out or order in?" Once again, there seemed to be another layer to the question. Addison looked around, her gaze landing on the couch. If they ate in, would he lay her down on that couch? She was supposed to be here for something other than an afternoon quickie, but suddenly the concept seemed to be one she could get on board with.

No. You are here to talk *to him.* "I can run out and get something. I didn't even pause to think about the fact I might be interrupting."

"I'm due for a break. All the emails and negotiations are threatening to make my eyes cross." He moved around the desk and pulled her into his arms. "Besides, I'm never going to say no to more time with you."

Easy for him to say. Or even for *her* to say. The truth of the matter was that work ruled both their lives. Her company was functioning just fine without her right now, but she couldn't be gone indefinitely. Funny, but the thought of flying back to New York didn't hold the appeal it had three days ago. If she was back home, she couldn't stop by Caine's work at the drop of a hat just because she missed the feeling of his presence filling up the room.

God, what was she going to do?

Caine stopped her from descending into a truly dramatic freak-out by handing her a take-out menu. "Pick what you'd like and I'll have Agnes order it."

"I'm not sure that's the best idea. She doesn't like me very much. She might poison it." Addison laughed, but she wasn't completely joking.

"It'll be fine."

Caine spoke like it was already decided, and why wouldn't he? He was king and this was his kingdom. She doubted the idea of someone defying his wishes even crossed his mind. He simply expected to be obeyed and was.

Much like now. She glanced over the Chinese menu, and went with her usual—beef and broccoli.

Addison took a seat on the couch while Caine called the front office and gave their order. She ran her finger along the seam. This piece of furniture really was quite comfortable— she could almost see how he'd managed to justify sleeping here so many nights.

But his bed was a thousand times better. She smiled at the thought. She would think that, wouldn't she? She hadn't spent much time actually sleeping on the mattress, but her experiences had most definitely been memorable.

Caine took a seat next to her, close enough that they touched from knee to hip. He stretched his arms across the back of the couch, practically inviting her to lean against him. She didn't hesitate to take him up on the silent offer. Addison hated the confusion coloring everything about her time with him. The only way to silence the doubts eating away at her was to touch him.

He let loose a breath. "Damn, darlin', I think I missed you."

She didn't know if that was a comfort or something more she had to worry about that they were on the same page, but her personal issues couldn't hold up against the feel of him against her. She breathed in his scent. "It doesn't seem like you should miss a person after only a few hours." He went tense against her, so she couldn't leave it at that. "But I missed you, too."

"I can't say I hate to hear that."

There was something there in his tone, something too impossible to put into words. If she let them have this quiet moment, it might surface, and she suspected things would never be the same. "Since you asked me an uncomfortable question last night, I'd like to return the favor."

He smoothed down her hair, but didn't look too worried. "Ask."

"Is this really what you want to do?"

"This being…"

He was going to be difficult—as usual. "This being CEO of McNeill Enterprises—and everything that comes with it in regard to your father and family." It was a legacy position, which meant he hadn't chosen it for himself. She'd known that going in. What she *hadn't* known was what he would have chosen if things had played out differently—like if *he* were the younger son, instead of Brock.

"Not pulling your punches, are you?"

"No more than you were last night." She *still* didn't have a satisfactory answer when it came to the thoughts he'd put in her head. But she wasn't about to admit as much to him, no matter how good he made her feel. If Caine realized how confused and off-center he had her right now, he wouldn't hesitate to capitalize on it.

"Touché." He leaned back, letting go of the tension riding his body—and putting a little bit of distance between them. "I don't know."

Addison blinked. She'd expected him to tell her that

she had no idea what she was talking about. Or kiss her to distract her. Or really, do anything but basically acknowledge that he was as confused about his life as she currently felt. She searched his face and, for once, those gray eyes were open to her. "You really don't know."

"Up until recently, if you asked me that question, I would have told you that this is exactly what I wanted to do—what I've always wanted to do. I'm not so sure anymore."

Caine wasn't the type of man to waffle about something he felt so strongly about. "What changed?"

He met her gaze. "I had this matchmaker show up on my doorstep and whip through my life like a tornado. She even got me a dog."

"A wonderful dog with a majestic past." He'd warm up to Gollum and her pups eventually. She hoped.

"Noted." He rolled his shoulders. "This path has been laid out for me from birth. If Brock was less inclined to tell our father where to shove his expectations, there might have been a choice, but my brother's heart has never been with McNeill Enterprises."

No, Brock's heart lay elsewhere. Since he'd founded one of the most successful nonprofit organizations that benefited women and children in abusive households, she thought he'd made the right choice. That man had been wasted in his father's company.

But she was less concerned with his heart than with Caine's. "Is yours?"

"That's the question, isn't it? I like my job. I like handling the deals and working to expand the company. The hours never bothered me before, but you might have had a point about sleeping so many nights on this couch." He patted the cushion.

Aha. Not that she needed to be told her instincts were right, but it was still nice to hear him admit it. "They're the same hours your dad worked, aren't they?" Still worked, if his showing up at Caine's house was any indication.

"Yeah, and do you know how many of my sports games or debates he made?" He went on before she answered— not that she needed to. Working from early in the morning until late at night didn't exactly leave room for anything else. "None. Not a single damn one."

"I'm sorry."

"That's why I wasn't planning on settling down anytime soon. I saw how things developed between my parents. My old man was always more married to the company than he ever was to my mother. If I can't have a damn dog, how am I supposed to have a wife?" While she was still trying to process that, he kept going. "But now you've just got me thinking about a wife and kids, and wondering how much time I'm willing to sacrifice at the altar of McNeill Enterprises."

Her heart tried to skip a beat before reality set in. She'd succeeded in bringing him around to thinking about those things—that didn't mean he was thinking about them with *her*.

But…what if he was?

Longing hit her so hard, she nearly curled into a ball. What would it be like to have kids with Caine? To create a big family to fill up that ridiculously large house? It was a fight not to press her hand to her stomach. She'd always wanted children—at least four of them—but that dream had died with Aiden.

Caine's question from earlier circled back through her head. What would she tell that fictional man who wanted kids? She shifted, not liking the direction her thoughts had taken, and realized he was staring at her. Crap. "Did you figure that answer out?"

"To some extent. I want kids, darlin'. A bunch of them." She shivered at the intent in his eyes. Intent directed at *her*. "I want a wife who I get to actually come home to. And, unlike my father, I'm sure as fuck not going to miss any of those special moments and occasions. I'm going to be there."

She swallowed hard. *Focus on the conversation. Take everything at face value. Ignore the panic.* "It sounds like that's mutually exclusive with the job you hold now."

"With the way my old man would have me do it? Definitely."

And that was the crux of the matter. From what she could tell, he'd practically killed himself throughout his entire life to get his father's attention and make the man proud. Was he really going to throw that all away? It was easy to declare his intentions when there was no wife or children demanding his precious time.

Would his resolve last past the fantasy and into the reality?

Chapter Sixteen

Caine could barely take his eyes off Addison as they ate. He'd never seen her in anything other than dresses, and while he loved the fact that they showed off her legs, seeing her in jeans was something else altogether. The denim was faded from countless washings, and it clung to her like a comfortable second skin. It was as if she'd let down a layer of armor simply by putting them on.

He spoke without thinking. "Would you like to play hooky?"

"I thought you were in the middle of some crisis."

He was, but he had the feeling that if he let her walk out of here after their meal without figuring out where her head was, he'd lose her. It was a sacrifice he wasn't willing to make. "I can spare a few hours."

"Who are you, and what have you done with Caine McNeill?"

"Very funny."

She glanced at the door. "Are you sure your resident prison guard isn't going to call your dad and report you?"

Agnes probably would. She loved Caine, but she was loyal to the company first. "I'll cross that bridge when I come to it." The deal wouldn't explode in the next few hours, and for the first time in living memory, he was almost as desperate to get out of these four walls as he was to spend more time with Addison.

"If you're sure."

"I am." He took her hand. "Come on."

Agnes rose when they came through the door, her gaze jumping from Caine to Addison and back again. "You're leaving?"

"I'll be back in a few hours." He stopped in front of the elevator. "Hold all my calls from everyone except Gloucester."

"What about your father?"

The elevator doors opened and he guided Addison in. "Hold calls from him, too." It would piss the old man off, but his wrath could wait until Caine was back in the office.

The doors closed and Addison started to step away. He refused to have any more distance between them, physical or otherwise, so he pulled her back into his arms. "What would you like to do?"

"I'd actually like to go out to Old Stone Fort."

That was exactly the last thing he expected her to say. "Really?"

She glanced at him. "Yeah, why not?"

"I assumed that since you're from New York and friends with Regan, you'd share her hatred of everything nature-related."

She laughed. "Hardly. Unlike her, I'm not afraid of squirrels.

I actually grew up in upstate New York, so I'm no stranger to the forest."

It was something else he hadn't known about her. "If you wear those shoes on the hiking trails, you're liable to break an ankle."

"I have tennis shoes in the car." When he stared, she shrugged. "I was already planning on checking out the Old Stone Fort this afternoon. It's got a fascinating history, and it'd be silly to spend time in this area of Tennessee without driving down and seeing it at least once."

It was something he'd seen enough times that it had lost its charm. It seemed like a lot of things had lost their charm since he hit adulthood. "You certainly are prepared." He followed her to her car, and nearly got hit in the face with a set of keys. "*Shit.*"

"Sorry. I thought you were paying attention." Funny, but she didn't look the least bit sorry. "You know where it is and, let's be honest, I'm not the greatest driver these days. We might as well kill two birds with one stone."

She wouldn't have much reason to get behind the wheel, living in the city. Damn it, he should have thought of that and assigned her a driver. "My driving skills are at your command then."

They headed out of town, a comfortable silence filling the car. Was she still thinking about what he'd asked her last night? He checked the urge to press her on the subject, since it wouldn't do anything but create strife between them. She was thinking about it, had been since they talked about it, if her comment earlier was any indication. He had to let her work it out on her own or she'd instinctively dig in her heels.

The Old Stone Fort had been around for as long as

anyone could remember. Caine had gone out there for a field trip with his junior high history class once, if he remembered correctly. It had been built by prehistoric Native Americans, and there was some debate over exactly how old the fort was and what its history might mean, but what really drew people these days were the handful of gorgeous hiking trails that circled through the area, giving great views of the various falls from the rivers that connected to make the Ancient Indian Enclosure into a peninsula. There were also camping grounds, but his family had never been into that sort of thing, so he didn't have much experience with it.

Fall had turned the trees' leaves a rich array of warm colors, making the drive even prettier than normal. Since it was in the middle of a weekday, they pretty much had the parking lot to themselves as he pulled into an empty space.

Addison had already kicked off her heels and laced up her tennis shoes. She didn't wait for him to come around to open her door before she jumped out of the car. "This is beautiful."

He shrugged out of his suit jacket and looked around. "Yeah, I suppose it is."

"Do you come here often?"

He unbuttoned his cuffs and rolled up his sleeves. If he'd stopped to think about it, he would have driven by the house first to change. The clothing he wore was more suitable to conducting business meetings than hiking through the woods, no matter how sedate the trails were. "It's not really my thing."

She laughed and laced her hand through the crook of his arm, guiding him toward the trailheads next to the museum. "If I went by your questionnaire, you don't really have a lot of 'things' beyond work."

That had been the truth for the entirety of his adult life. Now he wanted something different. "I'm looking to change that." He covered her hand with his free one, anchoring her to him.

They bypassed the museum and started down the trail. It was quieter here, almost as if they'd stepped into a different time. The trees whispered with the faint breeze, the sound not quite enough to cover up the crunch of their footsteps on the scattering of leaves over the path.

She let out a breath. "Thank you for coming with me. I don't mind walking alone but it's nice to have company."

And that was just it. She walked every trail—metaphorically or otherwise—alone. He did as well, but that didn't mean he wasn't going to jump at the chance to change. "You don't have to."

"Hmmm?"

"You don't have to do it alone." He felt the tension in her body, but kept going. As many times as he'd promised himself that he wouldn't push her, he couldn't shake the feeling that she'd let this opportunity pass if it meant she didn't have to face certain ugly truths. He couldn't let that happen. He refused to. "You could do it with me."

"I *am* doing it with you. Right now, in fact."

It was tempting to leave it at that and maintain the fragile balance they'd created, but Caine had decided last night that he wasn't willing to let Addison walk out of his life without a fight. "I don't mean right this second, and you know it. Addison, I care about you."

She stopped walking, carefully removing her hand from his arm. "You know how I feel about soul mates."

"I do." And he'd change her mind if he could—a fact he suspected they both knew. "I'm not asking you to marry me." *Not yet.*

"Then what *are* you asking me?"

Here was the moment where it would all come together into a new future or fall apart in ruins around him. "I'm asking you to give this—us—a real shot, and stop fighting the connection between us."

"I see." She shook her head. "No pressure, then."

"I know what I want—you. And I know you want me, too. I also know that you've been through a hell of a lot in your life and it's making you skittish. I can respect that."

A faint smile pulled at the edges of her lips. "Not that you'd let my so-called issues stop you."

That was an argument for another day. Right now, all he wanted was to get her to take that first step. "I'm not going to tattoo my name on your ass. I'm asking you to be my girlfriend."

"Girlfriend." She said the word like she was tasting it.

He also wanted her to stay, but this wasn't a good time to bring that up. Caine had a feeling if he piled too much onto her, she'd rabbit on sheer instinct. So he had to take this slowly and carefully. He held out his hand. "What do you say?"

"It's not going to work. We're not soul mates." Except she didn't sound so sure when she said that.

"Life has a way of surprising us, darlin'. All I'm asking for is a chance."

"Then why does it feel like such a big deal?" She edged closer, her arms wrapped tightly around herself.

Because it *was* a big deal. Neither one of them started

relationships lightly, and with good reason. "The unknown is always scary. Luckily, you won't be facing it alone." He crooked his fingers. "What do you say? Will you take that jump with me?"

The feeling of her hand slipping into his was perfection. He didn't haul her closer or kiss her senseless, though he wanted to. Instead, he squeezed her hand and placed it back on the crook of his arm. She took that first step with him down the trail, and he didn't comment on the way her hand shook where she touched him, and she didn't comment on the fact that he was grinning like a fool.

Things were finally starting to come together.

Chapter Seventeen

Addison chose the most responsible dress she owned. She couldn't remember the last time she'd been so obsessed with what to wear, but this was twice in three days. She wasn't a fan of this new habit, but tonight she was officially meeting Caine's parents. After that incident with his father, it paid to be a little paranoid when it came to putting herself together for dinner. He was the kind of man who judged someone at first sight, and never gave a second thought about it.

Knowing what she did about Mr. McNeill, she didn't like her chances of changing whatever assumptions he'd already made about her.

She refused to call Regan a second time for advice. She could do this. She'd been impressing strangers ever since she started her matchmaking business. Most people came through her doors with a healthy degree of skepticism. She didn't get to be as prominent as she was in New York without learning to combat such things. Compared to some of her more problematic clients, this dinner should be a piece of cake.

Should being the operative word.

Her phone rang as she was pinning the curl into place. She carefully nudged the curling iron away from the edge of the counter and answered. "Yes?"

"Don't kill me."

Caine sounded so resigned, she wanted to reach through the phone and hug him. "You're running late?" She smiled. "Now, why don't I find that surprising?"

"I'll make it up to you as soon as I get there."

Problematic schedules were the norm when it came to men like him—men who always had one disaster or another waiting on the horizon. Since he'd taken the afternoon with her, she wasn't particularly surprised that something had happened. But that didn't change the fact that, when presented with a choice between her and work—a choice she never would have put to him—he'd chosen *her*. "When are your parents supposed to be here?"

"Five thirty."

She leaned her head out the bathroom door and bit back a groan. "That's in twenty minutes."

"I'm getting out of here as soon as I can—promise."

Caine and his promises. He seemed to genuinely mean every one of them—he hadn't broken one since she met him, so she doubted he would start today. Addison took a deep breath and pushed away the nagging sensation that she'd bitten off more than she could chew. He'd been consistent the entire time they'd spent together. That wasn't going to magically change just because they were in new territory. "I can handle things until you get here."

"I know you can. I'll see you soon."

She hung up, a mess of conflicting feelings coursing through her. She slipped on her heels—one didn't meet one of the most powerful couples south of the Mason-Dixon line without shoes on—and headed downstairs. Caine had brought in a chef tonight to prepare dinner for them. She told him she was more than capable of cooking and entertaining, but he got this look on his face that told her arguing wasn't going to get her anywhere. His parents were coming and therefore a chef would cook dinner. It was just the way things were done.

This was his rodeo, so she let him have his way. It didn't stop her from checking on the chef he'd hired, though. The man shooed her out of the room almost immediately, but not before she caught a whiff of whatever he was cooking. It smelled decadent.

Exiled from the kitchen, she wandered through the house, Gollum at her heels and the four pups trailing after. The piano called to her—it was one of the nicest she'd ever played on—but she couldn't afford to get caught up in the music tonight. The dog pushed her head into Addison's hand, obviously sensing some of her nervousness. "It's okay, girl. I'm just feeling out of sorts."

Caine wanted her to be his girlfriend. He'd been very, very careful to not ask for more than that, but she'd seen the intent on his face. He was playing for keeps, and he had his eye on her as the prize.

A shiver worked its way through her body. All he wanted was a chance. She could do that. Hell, she'd already agreed to give him that. A small part of her rebelled at the idea, but the rest of her wanted him too much to deny herself as

much time with him as physically possible. They hadn't talked about details or how this thing would work with them,
but she cared about him too much to walk away just because
she was scared. She was going to give it her best shot.

That's all she could do, right?

She gave Gollum's head one last stroke and opened the
back door to let her and her pups out. Addison had a feeling
that tonight would be tension-filled enough without adding
a dog who already didn't like George McNeill to the mix.

She barely made it back to the bottom of the stairs when
the doorbell rang. Addison glanced at the watch on her wrist.
Five thirty, to the minute. She might not be particularly close
with her parents in recent years, but when they visited they
never used the doorbell. The fact that his parents did—and
waited for someone to answer—was strange.

She swung the heavy wooden door open, keeping her
professional smile in place, and took in the picture they
made—almost as if they'd posed on purpose. Having met
both the McNeill boys, it wasn't hard to see where they got
their looks. They shared his broad shoulders, square jaw, and
dark coloring, though their father's hair was completely sil-
ver. It only served to make him appear even more distinguished.

Mrs. McNeill didn't seem to have a blond hair out of
place. Everything about her was poised and graceful, despite
the fact that she wasn't actually moving. She had the kind
of face that put her anywhere between thirty and fifty, and
Addison didn't detect any of the perpetual artificial surprise
that came from Botox injections.

God, they got excellent genetics from both sides of the
family.

Realizing she was being rude by staring, she brightened her smile and offered her hand. "Mr. McNeill. Mrs. McNeill. I'm Addison St. Claire." Technically, she'd introduced herself to him the other night, but she would happily block the whole experience from her memory if possible. She hoped he'd give her the courtesy of doing the same.

"I remember."

Apparently not. She tried not to notice that he barely touched her hand before he withdrew, and his wife followed suit. This might be more difficult than she had anticipated, but she told Caine she'd try, so that was exactly what she was going to do. "The chef has put together something truly marvelous."

"No, not yet." He looked around, as if expecting his son to pop out of the woodwork. "Where's Caine? I tried to call him today and apparently he was out of the office. I don't suppose you would know something about that?"

She'd have to be a fool to step between father and son, but that didn't stop her from wanting to. Caine worked insane hours and set aside any social life he might have had—wanted or not—for his father's approval. The least the man could do was give it to him. But she knew better—if he hadn't done something to be proud of in the thirty-five years of his life to date, she doubted he'd start now. George McNeill was the kind of miserable man who was never satisfied with anything anyone did, least of all his sons.

So she smiled and ushered them farther into the house because there was nothing else to do. "You'll have to ask him about that. He's running a little late—I'm sure you know how that is, sir—but he should be here shortly."

"If he'd been in his office this afternoon like he was

supposed to, he wouldn't be running late now."

Mrs. McNeill gave a sigh, turning in a slow circle to take in the room. "Oh, George, I truly miss this place."

"It's not ours anymore." He glared at Addison like this was her fault. "It was time for our son to start his own family, and the only way that's going to happen is if he's here on his own."

Addison tried to process all the facts and undertones she heard from that pointed comment. From the research she'd done, she'd known this was the McNeill family seat, but hadn't really registered that this is the house Caine had grown up in. She paged through her memory of each room, trying to figure out where he and Brock must have played... and came up with nothing. Everything about this house was geared to adults. What was it like growing up in a house that seemed to have no place for children?

No wonder he hadn't been eager to start a family of his own. With these two as his parents, she couldn't imagine a childhood full of warmth.

As they followed her into the formal dining room, Caine's mother spoke up again. "What is it you do, Addison?"

She'd gotten all sorts of reactions when she told people what she did for a living—from the amused to the intrigued to the downright mean. Somehow, she didn't think she was going to get a good response from either of these people. "I'm a matchmaker. I own my own company up in New York City."

"A matchmaker? Is there much market for that sort of thing these days?"

She tried to remind herself this wasn't a new question. She'd answered it half a million times since she started

Connected at the Lips. "You'd be surprised. It's difficult to meet people despite technology making the world a smaller place. I just help some people connect the dots."

Mr. McNeill scoffed. "It sounds like you're a glorified pimp."

"George!"

Addison met his gaze and it was everything she could do not to drop her eyes. "I am many things, sir, but a pimp is not one of them. There's nothing wrong with helping two people find each other."

He didn't blink. "If that's true, and you're so successful up in the city, then what the hell are you doing down here messing around with our son?"

She knew she should keep silent, but she didn't like the direction his thoughts were apparently headed. "I'm down here at the request of a friend to help Caine."

"And this friend of yours asked you to sleep with him? Tell me again how you're not a pimp."

Her spine was so straight it felt like it might crack in two. "I don't have to explain myself to you."

"Now see here, girl, that's where you'd be wrong. You're in *my* house, with *my* son, screwing with *my* corporation. I'm the *only* person you have to explain yourself to right now."

Mrs. McNeill looked ready to pass out. "George, please!"

"You just got done saying that this is Caine's house."

"He lives here now, but this property and his home are owned by McNeill Enterprises. I'm surprised you didn't know that, considering all the research you must've done before you took him on." He stepped closer, getting right in her face. "Any matchmaker worth her salt would do research on a client before taking them on. I don't see how you managed to keep a big fancy company up in New York City if you weren't at least somewhat competent. Which means you knew my son has a hell of a lot of money before you came down here."

For all his bluster, it sounded like Mr. McNeill had been doing some research of his own. Addison crossed her arms over her chest and lifted her chin. "If I was looking for a man with money, it wouldn't require traveling all the way to Tennessee."

"Be that as it may, one has to wonder if you sleep with all your clients, or just the rich ones."

Now even Mrs. McNeill had stopped trying to quiet her husband down and seemed to be waiting for an answer. Addison wanted to throw up her hands and scream. This is why she didn't sleep with clients, though Caine had stopped being a client nearly as soon as he'd become one in the first place. But how was she supposed to explain that to his parents? Neither of them seemed particularly inclined to be forgiving in this situation.

She was saved—or maybe cursed—from answering by the sound of the front door opening. Footsteps echoed through the hall as they stood and waited for Caine to make his way to them. He took in the room at a glance, and crossed over to slip his arm around Addison's waist. "Mother, Father. It's good to see you."

And that's when things started to really go downhill.

• • •

Caine should have known better than to work late today of all days—his father was bound to be pissed because he'd been avoiding his calls. But he was on his way out the door when Richards himself called, angry over concessions he'd made to keep Gloucester from backing out. It'd taken an hour to calm the man down, and by that point, there was no way he could avoid being late. He'd known his parents wouldn't be pleased, but he didn't expect to walk into the room and find them ready to lynch Addison. His old man's face was so red, he looked like he was in danger of bursting an artery.

Before he could ask what the hell was going on, his mother pointed a shaking finger at them, her face pale beneath her tan. "You're... You're sleeping with this woman?"

They'd devolved to "this woman"? Shit was worse off than he'd thought. "I'm doing a good bit more than sleeping with her. We're dating." They may have been officially doing so for only about six hours, but the intent was there, and that's all that mattered to him.

As he suspected, though, it was exactly the wrong thing to say. His mother practically wailed. "What in God's name are you thinking, Caine? She lives in New York. A woman like that doesn't move down here—she just doesn't. Are you leaving us?"

Well, shit. She'd nearly had a breakdown when Brock moved away. It had taken countless promises not to follow in his younger brother's footsteps before she'd finally stopped making dramatic comments about every man in their family abandoning her. "No, Mom, I'm not moving away. Please calm down."

"You damn well better not be moving." If anything, his father's face got even redder. "You've been fucking around on this deal because of this little piece of tail, and it ends now."

"Don't talk about her like that." He stared his old man down, willing him to take it back or, at the very least, shut the fuck up.

Caine should have known better.

"Unlike you, I call things as I see them. She's little better than a gold digger and you've obviously been spending too much time with that lazy piece of work that is your brother. You're starting to act like him instead of the man the heir to McNeill Enterprises needs to be."

His father was willing to throw away thirty-five years of Caine trying to please him the first time he actually stood up for himself and the woman he cared about? It shouldn't have been a surprise, and it sure as fuck shouldn't have hurt, but apparently he was a slow learner when it came to family.

Nothing he did would ever be good enough for his father.

Realizing that made him so goddamn tired. What was it all for? His dad should want him to be independent and happy. Yes, he should be able to juggle that while pushing McNeill Enterprises to the next level, but those two elements had never even factored into what his father considered a success. If he wasn't doing things exactly like his old man—down to the smallest detail—then he was failing.

There was a time when he used to love this job, but it had been years since he truly felt that way. To have his father trying to sabotage the first good thing to walk into his life... No fucking way. "You're right, Dad. It does end now. I quit."

There were three gasps in the room, but was Addison who spoke first. "You can't quit."

"Aha! I knew you just wanted him for his money." His father turned on him. "But the woman's right—you can't quit.

You're the CEO of McNeill Enterprises."

"So find a new one." The more he thought about it, the freer he felt. If he wasn't the CEO, his life was his own for the first time. He could do anything. He could go back to school. He could move somewhere else... Like even New York City. "I think it's best you two leave."

"This isn't the last of this conversation."

Each breath he took felt freer than the last. "That's the beauty of quitting, Father. It actually *is* the end of this conversation."

His old man pinned him with a glare, and then sent an even more vicious one in Addison's direction. "You'll be hearing from me." Then he took his wife's arm and led her out of the room.

Even then, Caine didn't take a full breath until he heard the front door slam shut. "That went well."

Chapter Eighteen

That went *well*?

Addison was afraid to move her head to look at Caine. How in God's name could he have thought that went well? His parents thought she was a prostitute who was going to steal him away, and he responded by confirming all their fears and telling them he was going to quit his job. That was so far from *well*, it wasn't even in the same universe. In reality—or at least her reality—this had been nothing short of a disaster.

Finally able to move, she shoved his arm from her waist. "What the hell is wrong with you?"

"Wrong with me? I thought you'd be happy."

Which proved he didn't really know her at all. However he felt about the lack of free time, he cared about his job. Maybe he didn't like everything that came along with it, or the constant pressure from his father, but he enjoyed the challenge of it. She'd have to be deaf, blind, and mute not to hear it in his voice when he talked about putting these deals together. For him to quit because of her? Absolutely not.

"Call your father right now and apologize."

Caine jerked back, his gray eyes going wide. "I'm not fucking apologizing. *He* should apologize. He insulted you."

"Yes, he did. I was handling it. I didn't need you to act like a rampaging caveman in response." This was just proving her original theory right. They might match up really well in the bedroom, but true soul mates matched up in other areas as well. Even if there was more than one soul mate per person, there was no way Caine could be hers. And, damn it, as much she didn't want to leave, it was painfully obvious that as long she stayed here, he wouldn't search out his rightful soul mate.

And he'd keep sabotaging his life as a result. Just like Grandmother had warned the last time she'd tried to prove the soul mate theory wrong. Caine might have feelings for her now, but the longer she stayed here, the uglier things would get between them, until they hated each other.

Which meant she had to leave as soon as she possibly could, no matter how much it hurt.

Caine looked ready to shake her. "You can't seriously expect me to sit back and let him talk to you like that."

"I can fight my own battles. I always have." Ever since Aiden died, anyways.

As if sensing her thoughts, he closed in on her. "You don't have to. That's the whole point of sharing your life with someone—you get to lean on them when you need it."

Which was more attractive than she would ever admit aloud. Addison sidestepped his reach. If she let him touch her now, he'd kiss her, and then it would be all over. She'd forget all the reasons why this thing between them wouldn't work, and she'd cheat him out of his chance at finding true happiness.

That got her moving when nothing else would have. She couldn't do that to him. She couldn't be that selfish. Already, her being here had disrupted his life in the worst way possible. All she'd been trying to do was help him, and she'd managed to piss off his father and get him to quit his job inside of two weeks. It would be impressive if it weren't so terrifying. There was only one way to fix this, and that was to leave.

So she backed up, her head held high. "I'm going to my room."

He froze, gray eyes searching her face. She forced herself to give him nothing. "Just like that? You're done with the conversation, so it's over?"

She wasn't done, not until she'd put the final nail in the coffin that was their fledgling relationship, but she couldn't do that while in the room with him. "We can talk more tomorrow if it would make you feel better."

"It would make me feel better to talk right now."

Well, that was just too damn bad. "I need some space to think things over." With that, she turned around and marched out of the room, determined to put as much space between them as possible. Even this entire empty house wasn't enough, but there was no help for it. She locked herself into her bedroom and snagged her computer off the nightstand. From there, it was quick work to find the number she was looking for. She dialed before she could talk herself out of it.

"This is Brenda Nickle."

Her breath left her in a whoosh. "Brenda, it's Addison."

"So great to hear from you. What have you got for me? Please tell me he's a cowboy who wears Wranglers and doesn't believe in shirts." Brenda had been a client for nearly six months, and gone on quite a few dates, but nothing had clicked yet. She was damn near perfect for Caine—poised and polished with a wicked sense of humor.

Her heart tried to lodge itself in her throat, but she managed to croak out, "Not a cowboy, but he's from Tennessee and has an accent that will make your knees weak."

"Sounds like my kind of man. When do I meet him?"

Addison gave her the details, promising to have her on the first flight the next morning. She did some quick math in her head—that would put the woman on their doorstep around eight. Just in time to kill any chance of her and Caine being together.

· · ·

Caine was tempted to hunt Addison down as soon as he woke up, but he made himself take a shower and get ready first. The acts did nothing to cool his temper, but they gave him the distance to realize he needed to take a step back and listen to what was bothering her. Though she had damn well better get used to him defending her from assholes—even if that asshole was his father.

He headed downstairs, frowning when the first strains of piano echoed through the corridor. Why was she playing that song again? He'd looked up the lyrics of the original version after she told him the title, and it was so damn sad. Knowing she picked it specifically made his chest feel hollow.

An unfamiliar woman's voice stopped him just outside the room. "That's beautiful, Addison. I didn't know you could play."

"I don't do it often."

What the hell was going on here? A sneaking suspicion wormed through him, but he told himself he was jumping at shadows. Surely she hadn't brought in another goddamn woman...

There was only one way to find out. He took a deep breath, feeling like he was about to step onto a battlefield, and walked through the door. Addison once again sat on the piano bench, her fingers playing over the keys. She didn't look up as he walked over. "This is Brenda Nickle. She's flown down from Philadelphia to meet you."

Jesus fucking Christ. "Why are you doing this?" After everything they'd gone through, he was sure that he'd gotten through to her. Last night wasn't the best of evenings, but what his parents thought of her didn't matter in the least to him. All Caine cared about was how *he* felt about her.

Except apparently, even after everything, she didn't feel the same way. There was no other explanation for why she had flown yet another woman down here to date him. He didn't even glance at the woman. "Answer me, Addison."

She finally looked up, and the shadows in her eyes staggered him. "Because it's the only way. I had my chance at a soul mate. You should have yours, too."

"Careful there, darlin', you're clinging to that soul mate bullshit so hard, your fear is showing through." Because that's what this was—she was afraid. That was the only explanation that made sense when he looked back over the last week.

"It's not bullshit." She took a shuddering breath and carefully lowered the cover over the piano keys. "I can't change the way I feel. And I don't feel like that with you."

"Liar." She jumped, but he didn't relent. "You aren't willing to at least *try* with me, which makes me wonder what scares you more. That we won't work out—or that we will?"

"We won't work. Last night proved that. Your father insults me, so you quit your job like a pouty child throwing a tantrum." She carefully stood. "I won't be the reason you ruin your life, especially when it's not meant to be between us."

He wanted to prove her wrong. Hell, he'd been fighting *so damn hard* to do just that, and she was shooting him down before he got a word out. "I didn't quit my job for you."

The delicate sound of a feminine throat clearing broke through. "Uh, do you want me to leave?"

He leaned back and crossed his arms, staring at Addison. "I've been fighting tooth and nail to get you to consider being with me, so you need to tell me the truth for once. Is it all for nothing? Is this something you're never going to get over? Say the word and I'll take *her* out." He held his breath, waiting for her answer.

She lifted her chin, her dark eyes giving nothing away. "I think Brenda would be an excellent match for you."

Fuck. She wasn't going to back down, and he wasn't fool enough to continue beating his head bloody on the brick wall that was Addison. "Fine. Have it your way. Let's go, Brenda." Without another word, he turned and stalked out the door. He made it three steps before he slowed down so the woman trailing behind him could catch up.

She didn't say anything until they crossed the threshold

of the front door. "I might be a little slow on the uptake, but I get the feeling there's something going on between you two."

"Not anymore." Even as angry as he was, he couldn't stop himself from holding the Jaguar's door open for her. It wasn't *her* fault that his life was falling apart around him.

He gunned it and tore out of the driveway. Damned difficult woman. What was she so afraid of? They had a good fucking thing going between them and she'd just thrown it all away under the flimsiest excuse she could come up with.

Quitting his job might have been impulsive, but it wasn't like he didn't have other options. He just needed to sit down and figure out what they were. There was no reason to throw the baby out with the bathwater just because things had gotten a little bumpy.

Caine made it to the first light inside the city limits before it hit him. She'd made her excuses—just like she had been doing since they met—and he'd just left. He'd told her that he'd fight for her, and the first time she got scared and started talking about how it would never work, he went and proved her right.

"Christ." He looked at the woman in the passenger seat. She was classically gorgeous, even with her caramel hair blown a thousand different ways by the drive. She deserved better than to have been used as a pawn in the ongoing thing between them. "I'm sorry you got dragged into this."

She smoothed her hair back and lifted her sunglasses so she could meet his gaze. "She's got you all twisted up in knots, doesn't she?"

He gave a strained smile. "Is it that transparent?"

"You're not exactly trying right now." She shrugged.

"I've known Addison a while now, and she deserves the best. If she's got you this messed up, you must really care for her."

He did. She was a giant pain in the ass and too stubborn by half, but she'd changed his life. "More than you can know."

Brenda rolled her eyes. "Yeah, I'm getting that. Then what are you waiting for? Put this monstrosity of a car through its paces and go get your woman."

Damn it, she was right. "You're a peach."

"Yeah, yeah. If you really want to thank me, I don't suppose you have a sexy friend around here you could hook a girl up with?"

He didn't, but he seemed to remember that Agnes had a son a few years younger than Caine. "I'll see what I can do." The light turned green and he practically burned rubber pulling a U-turn and flying back the way they'd come. It hadn't been that long. He'd sit Addison down and they'd figure things out. All it would take was one conversation.

Except when he screeched to a stop in front of his house, the first thing he heard was the damn dogs sending up a chorus of howls. Caine knew the truth even before he searched the house and came up empty.

Addison was gone.

Chapter Nineteen

Addison spent the next two days hiding. She paced her apartment, casting guilty looks at her closed computer, and ended up eating half a pint of Ben & Jerry's instead of opening it and facing the music. She'd just flat-out turned off her phone.

She couldn't handle it if Caine called. Or, worse in some ways, if he didn't.

And that didn't make a lick of sense. If she truly wanted him to be happy, she'd hope that he and Brenda hit it off and were even now planning their wedding and bushel of children.

But the very idea made her sick to her stomach.

She didn't know *what* she wanted. It was all so mixed up in her head and heart that she didn't know which way was up anymore. If she and Caine were doomed, then she'd done the right thing by leaving him before things ended up uglier than they already were. The weight in her chest only seemed to grow with each hour that passed. She wanted to see him, to have his arms around her, to see that unexpected wicked grin spread over his face.

A knock on her door had her heart leaping into her throat. She had plenty of friends, but she hadn't told anyone she was back from Tennessee yet — or that she'd jumped in a cab to the airport like a thief in the night as soon as Caine's car disappeared around the curve in the road.

She debated not opening it, but whoever was on the other side didn't seem to be willing to give up. With a sigh, she walked over and opened it.

Regan nearly bowled her over as she pushed her way into the apartment. "I thought so."

"How did you find me?"

"It really wasn't that hard. You've lived in this tiny apartment ever since I've known you. When Caine said you bolted, it didn't take a genius to deduct that this was where you'd hole up."

Her chest constricted at the sound of his name. "He called you."

"No, actually, he didn't. But Brock's mother did, along with Caine's secretary, and his head of staff. I didn't even know the McNeills had a head of staff for their freakishly large house down in that death trap of a forest, but I had to listen to Brock try to calm him down. Apparently there's a pack of wild dogs destroying everything." Regan propped her hands on her hips. "You bought him dogs."

"He needed to be more approachable." She sank onto the couch, her mind whirling. It was only then that she noticed the woman who had followed Regan through the door. "*Grandmother?*"

"Hello, dear."

This was too strange. She looked from one woman to the other. "I wasn't aware you two were acquainted."

"Regan reached out to me yesterday. Rather forcibly, I might add." She sank onto the couch next to Addison and took her hands. "What's this I hear about you and another young man?"

This was the conversation she'd been dreading. She already knew how it would play out, but she couldn't help saying, "I care about him, Grandmother. So much it feels like I can't breathe without him. I know it's wrong—"

Regan snorted. "Why don't we try that one again?"

Addison ignored her. "But it *felt* real. I've never felt like that before. I know he can't be my soul mate, but—"

"Wrong again."

She finally turned to glare at Regan. "Will you just shut up and let me talk?"

"Not when you're determined to sabotage the first chance you've had at happiness since I've known you. Caine's a big boy. So whatever you're over there mentally flogging yourself about, you can just let it go. He makes his own decisions—he always has."

That didn't make her feel the least bit better. "Why did you send me down there? You had to know this would blow up in my face and hurt both of us. I thought you knew everything."

She raised her eyebrows. "Everyone likes to throw that fact around when they're in a mess of their own making."

There it was. The truth. Addison was the one who'd made a mess of things. "You had to have known putting me in that house with him would complicate things."

"I'd hoped it would."

Addison pushed to her feet. "What the hell does that mean?" Had Regan really planned this?

"I'll tell you what I told your grandmother when I showed up on her doorstep yesterday." She crossed her arms over her chest. "You're wasting away. You're so damn miserable and you think if you just keep moving, it won't pull you under. It's bullshit. You don't honestly think I could sit back and watch you disappear on me—on all of us? Caine's right for you. You're just too stubborn to acknowledge it."

"He's not my soul mate. If I try to force a relationship with him knowing that, it will end horribly. Tell her, Grandmother." She waited, but the woman didn't seem inclined to jump in with a supportive comment. Addison turned to stare at her grandmother and frowned. She looked…uncomfortable. "What's going on?"

"Yes, Rose. Please tell your granddaughter what I found when I came knocking on your door at eight in the morning."

Grandmother didn't look up from her clasped hands. "I may have been…wrong."

Wrong? Addison shook her head, not comprehending. "Wrong about what?"

"All of it." She finally looked up. "I believed we only get one. I wouldn't have told you time and again if I didn't." She shot a nasty look at Regan. "And I stand by my opinion of that Lee fellow you contemplated trying things with before. He wasn't good for you. But…maybe this Caine is."

She blinked. Where the hell was this coming from? "I don't understand."

"It seems Grandma Rose has a suitor—one who answers the door in his bathrobe because he obviously stayed over."

Regan gave a victorious smile, oblivious to the fact that Addison's world was falling apart around her. "So you see, if your saintly grandmother gets a second chance at love—and you go, Grandma—then there's no reason *you* can't."

She couldn't deal with this. If that was true, it meant she'd ruined things with Caine *for no reason.* "You don't..." She threw up her hands. "Oh my God. You don't just get to crash into someone's life uninvited and start meddling."

Regan's smile dimmed. "What's the problem? I thought you'd be happy about this?"

"Happy? My grandmother has been *lying* to me. How is that making me happy?" She turned to Grandmother. "Why didn't you say something?"

She lifted her chin. "I'm not proud of keeping Roy from you—from all of you. He's a good man and he deserves better than that after six months."

Six months. "Then tell me *why.*"

"Because I was afraid. I don't like admitting it to you any more than I did to *her.*" She jerked her thumb at Regan. "After your grandfather died, a part of me died with him. I told you the truth when I said that I had tried to entertain other suitors and that it all came to naught. None of them could compare... Until now." She smiled and Addison went cold because she recognized that look. Her grandmother was in love. "He's wonderful. He makes me feel more alive than I have in decades. I feel like I have a second chance at life."

"I'm...happy for you." She was—or she would be if the loss of Caine weren't eating her up inside. She wanted to crawl into a hole because there was no cosmic force to blame like she'd been comforting herself with. No, it was just Addison, the one-woman disaster. She'd ruined things all on her own. "But that doesn't change what happened with Caine. His life is in ruins and for what? A potential relationship that was doomed before it got started."

Regan sank onto the arm of the couch across from her. "And who doomed it, Addison? Who was the one who wouldn't give him a damn chance when he asked for it, and then used the first excuse she could come up with to retreat back into her shell?"

She jerked back. "Don't you dare blame this on me. This is *your* fault. Both of your faults!" Then she realized she was pointing a finger at her best friend and her grandmother, and the burning in her chest only got worse. "God, what am I saying? I'm turning into a monster."

"No, honey. What you are is love struck. You never saw Caine coming, and that scares the shit out of you." Regan gave a faint smile. "I happen to know a thing or two about this kind of thing. Those McNeill men are sly when they want to be, and us New York women can be too stubborn for our own good."

"But…Aiden."

Grandmother took her hand. "Aiden was your husband and you loved him just as much as I loved your grandfather. But do you really think either of them would want us to stop living after their deaths? I put my life on hold for far too long because I believed—I *had* to believe—that each person got only one soul mate. I want better for you than that, honey."

"But—"

Regan took her other hand. "Would you have wanted him to be alone for the rest of his life if your positions were reversed?"

She opened her mouth to say there was no one else for her, but couldn't make herself speak. Of course she wouldn't want Aiden to stop living. He'd wanted kids as much as she had. It struck her that if the theoretical man in Caine's question had been Aiden, she wouldn't have even hesitated before telling him that he deserved a second chance at life. She took a gulping breath. "Oh, God."

"That's what I thought." Regan patted her hand. "I happen to know there's a flight to Nashville tomorrow. Why don't I book it for you?"

"He'll never forgive me for just leaving like that." She'd been such a shit in so many different ways, she wanted to go back in time and slap herself.

"You won't know until you try. Are you willing to miss your second chance?"

Hell no. If Caine told her to take a long walk off a short pier—and maybe she deserved that—then at least she'd know that she'd done everything she could to make it right. "I'll pack my things."

"That's what I thought."

Grandmother gave her hand another squeeze. "Go get him, honey."

. . .

Caine folded his hands and looked across the table at his father. It had taken his old man a full week to make an appearance. Frankly, if he had been taking bets, he would have wagered the man would never show up. Pride was something the McNeill family had in spades, himself included.

His father didn't look particularly happy to be having

this meeting, but he finally huffed out a breath and met Caine's gaze. "We need you."

The words came like a blow to the chest. He knew without bothering to sift through his memories that they had never come out of his father's mouth—especially not in regard to *him*. But he wasn't going to roll over and play dead just because his dad had finally decided to show a little appreciation. "I'm listening."

"I'm not as young as I used to be. Even if I was, your mother will leave me if I go back to the hours I was working before you took over." He shifted, seemed to realize he was doing it, and went still. "The company needs you as CEO. *I* need you as CEO."

Truth be told, the last week had been hell for him. It was something else Addison had been right about—he *did* enjoy his work. If there was some way to find a decent balance between it and the home life he currently didn't have, it would be an ideal situation. "If I'm going to consider coming back, there are conditions."

"What conditions?"

Part of him wondered why the hell he was bothering. Addison was gone. She'd made damn certain that he knew where he stood in her life—behind her dead husband. He didn't expect her to stop caring for the man, even if it had been seven years since his death, but if she couldn't admit that there was room in her life for someone else... Then she was right. There was no way they could make things work because she would see every fight or setback as further evidence that each person only got one blasted soul mate.

That didn't stop him from thinking about her. Nonstop. He'd taken to wandering the house at night, drifting through the rooms like he was one of the ghosts the locals claimed existed.

He felt like it more often than not.

Caine shook his head. He couldn't afford to mentally wander while negotiating with his father. Family or not, the old man would take him for everything he had if he didn't pay attention. "The hours, for one. There's no reason I can't delegate some of the paperwork so I can focus on the bigger picture." He held up his hand when his father started to speak. "I know it's not how things were done when you did it, but it's a changing world."

"If this is about that woman—"

"I'm going to stop you right there before you say something unforgivable." He took a deep breath, forcing calm into his body. Addison wasn't here. Getting furious on her behalf wasn't going to benefit anyone. It didn't stop him from wanting to beat something until the shitty feeling in his chest went away. "Regardless of whether it's Addison or another woman, at some point I *will* want to pursue a family."

"Continuing the McNeill name is vital."

The question rose again—had his father only had children so he'd have a built-in heir? Caine didn't give it voice. It didn't matter anymore. He knew what *he* was going to do, and that would have to be good enough. "When I have children, it's going to be for reasons beyond continuing our line—and I'm sure as fuck going to be a father to them."

His old man flinched. "Was that supposed to strike me down?"

He was so fucking tired. "Contrary to what you apparently believe, it's not always about you." He straightened the blank notepad in front of him. "I also want the ability to relocate."

"This *is* about that woman." When he tensed, his father laughed. "Well, hell, son. I never thought you'd be swayed by the fairer sex. That was always your brother's path."

Half a dozen responses rose within him, but he didn't give voice to any of them. Whatever he said at this point would come across as an excuse, and he sure as fuck wasn't going to touch the comment about Brock. "Do you agree to my terms?"

"You have me over a barrel and you know it."

Only because he refused to consider anyone without the McNeill name for the position. Caine waited, steepling his fingers. While his father thought it over, his mind wandered once again to Addison.

He'd looked up her matchmaking business and had spent entirely too much time staring at her picture on the About page. It was an old one, her hair cut differently than when she'd been down here, but her smile was the same. He'd even gone so far as to call the damn number, only to be informed that she was on vacation. The woman on the other end of the line refused to tell him when she'd be back. She'd shut off her personal phone, too.

For all intents and purposes, Addison had disappeared off the face of the earth.

She was in New York, but he couldn't exactly fly in and start going door to door. He *could* have asked Regan, but Caine wasn't sure she'd take his side. She could just as easily step in and block him from…going door to door or whatever half-assed plan he could come up with.

That didn't stop him from coming up with them.

Which just proved he needed to get his ass back to work, sooner rather than later. At least if he was in the office, he wouldn't be cruising airline sites for tickets from Nashville to New York.

His father cleared his throat. "Fine. We will do things your way." He pushed to his feet. "Now get your ass back in the office before Gloucester has a goddamn stroke." He turned and marched from the room.

Caine dropped his head into his hands. He'd won. This was exactly the balance he'd wanted to free up some of his time to pursue other things—to pursue a relationship with Addison. He should be over the moon that he'd accomplished it. But the crushing weight in his chest prevented it. What was the point? He couldn't imagine sharing his life with anyone but that pain-in-the-ass matchmaker, and she'd already proven that she was more inclined to cling to her martyr status than try to be happy.

He had nothing. Less than nothing, because now he knew exactly what he was missing in his life.

Well, fuck that. He wasn't about to sit back and let her get away. It was time for drastic measures.

Chapter Twenty

Addison swept through her apartment, looking for some indication that she'd forgotten something. The cab would be here in ten minutes, and she wanted to make sure she was at the curb and waiting. Her suitcase stood next to the door, ready to go. The only thing not completely ready was *her*. She stopped and took a deep breath. After Regan had left, she'd booked the first flight she could find to Nashville. It was just poor luck that it didn't leave until the next afternoon.

It didn't help that she was already kicking herself for waiting this long. A few days seemed like a small thing in the face of forever, but now that she could face the fact that she'd been totally and completely wrong, it was too much to be away from Caine. She wanted his arms around her and his voice rumbling in her ear.

But there was no telling if he'd take her back. She'd been singularly awful to him before she left, and he'd be totally justified in telling her to get out of his sight. Or, worse, that he wouldn't even see her.

She swallowed past the panic trying to take over. There was only one way to find out for sure what his reaction would be, and it was to get her ass on that plane and go apologize.

After one last glance to check the time, she opened her door and wrestled her suitcase through it. The elevator seemed to take forever, but she was reasonably sure that was only her nerves talking. The flight was going to be hell.

Outside, the brisk breeze made her wish she'd put on a heavier coat. *At least I'll only be outside for a few minutes.* She hefted the suitcase over a crack in the sidewalk and closer to the curb.

Somewhere nearby, a chorus of barking started up, painfully familiar. It was impossible, though. She'd left Gollum and her pups back in Tennessee. It was just a strange homesickness coming over her and making her think that some other dog sounded like them.

Her throat tried to close, but she forced herself to take another deep breath. She was going to make things right. It didn't matter if she'd left without saying good-bye. She was going back.

"Addison!"

What in the world? She turned and stumbled back a few steps at the sight of a tangle of white dogs. As they got closer, their barking increased in time with their pace, until they were dragging the person behind them. She followed the knotted leashes up to a body that had become nearly as familiar to her as her own. But it couldn't possibly be…

"Caine?"

He wrestled the dogs into submission inches away from

her legs. "You're here. I didn't know if I'd make it in time."

"In time?" She couldn't take her eyes off his face. Had it really been less than a week since she saw him last? It felt like a lifetime. "You're in New York." She tentatively reached out to pet Gollum's head. "You brought the dogs."

If he were anyone else, she would have said the expression on his face was...sheepish. "They're terrible road trip buddies."

He'd *driven* here? There were so many things she'd wanted to say to him, but now that he was standing in front of her, she couldn't find a single word. "I—"

"I shouldn't have let you leave." He took a step toward her, but had to instantly retreat, because the dogs started clamoring again. "You're the only one I want, and I let my anger get the best of me."

Why in God's name was he apologizing? He'd told her that he wanted her from the start. *She* was the one who'd made a mess of things. "I have the answer to the question you asked me back in your bar."

He'd had his mouth open—no doubt to keep apologizing for something that wasn't his fault to begin with—but he went still at her words. "I'm listening."

Her lower lip quivered and she made an effort to keep herself together. "I'd match him. I'd do everything I could to make sure he had a second chance at being happy." She moved closer, edging around one of the pups, and stopped just before she touched him. "I don't know how this thing with us will work. But... I think I love you, Caine. And that kind of thing doesn't come around often enough to just throw it away because it scares me."

"I missed you, darlin'." He transferred all the leashes to one arm and pulled her against him with the other. "So damn much."

She slipped her arms around him. "I missed you, too." The dogs caught sight of something they found interesting and lurched ahead, nearly taking Caine off his feet. She laughed. "We should get them inside before you lose that arm."

"Yeah." He winced. "We're going to have to find a house with a yard or a massive apartment, because five dogs in limited square footage will be a disaster."

Her heartbeat picked up. "What are you saying?"

"I've renegotiated with my father. You were right about my quitting, but I was able to get him to agree to let me delegate some of my responsibilities. And to relocate if I choose."

Relocate. He meant *here*. She smiled. "I hear New York is nice this time of year."

"Yeah." He looked around. "Nice and crisp. And the company can't be beat."

She threw her arms around him again. "I'm so sorry I was so terrible and blind and that I almost ruined things with us. Forgive me?"

"There's nothing to forgive. We all make mistakes." He glanced at the dogs. "They missed you, too, you know. They love you as much as I do."

He loved her. It was something she'd barely dared to hope. Addison kissed him, feeling like she could walk on the clouds. "I love you so much. Your being here feels too good to be true."

"It's just the beginning, darlin'. And I can promise you this—the best is yet to come."

Epilogue

Caine held Addison's hand as they climbed out of the cab, ready to catch her if she stumbled. She'd been doing that a hell of a lot more often these days, to the point where she'd given up the taller of her heels. Her growing stomach threw off her equilibrium, in addition to the cravings and morning sickness that she was only now, in the fifth month, moving past. "How do you feel?"

She pushed her hair back. "Like I could use some cake with extra frosting."

"I'll call in the order. Lemon filling, like usual?"

"Yes, please." She grinned up at him.

"Consider it done." He pulled her close and kissed her temple. He wasn't usually a man who obsessed over what a woman ate, but something about knowing that Addison was nurturing their child in her stomach changed everything. Part of it was the sheer pleasure she took in the food she was craving—the only other time he saw that look of ecstasy on her face was when he was inside her—but most of it was this primal need to take care of everything for her. He opened the door into the building. "You're certain you don't want to know what the baby is until we can pull together a gender reveal party?"

She stopped. "Don't you? We don't have to wait. I just thought it would be a fun idea."

"I want to." He kissed her to hide his sigh of relief. If she'd changed her mind in the last hour, he'd have to find a way to stall their going up to the condo. Surprising Addison was borderline impossible, but he'd enlisted Regan's help to make it happen. Slipping the doctor the instructions had made him feel like a novice spy, but it would be worth it if everything came together.

She pulled away with a laugh. "You know better than to get me started down here. We can have sex after I get my cake."

"Your priorities are skewed." He pushed the button for the elevator and used the movement to check his phone. A text from his sister-in-law waited.

We're good to go.

Thank God.

"On the contrary—my priorities are right where they should be. These days, food is the best kind of foreplay."

Caine followed her into the elevator, wondering for the first time if he'd made a terrible mistake. The only other time he'd surprised her was with his proposal, and even that hadn't been a complete surprise because Addison knew the moment they moved in together that it was coming. The wedding had been delightful, but she'd been the one steering that ship, and he was more than happy to do what made *her* happy.

This was something else.

She'd mentioned a gender reveal party last month when she was reading through one of her countless baby magazines, and how much she liked the idea of having their family and friends there to share the news with them as they found out. So he'd quietly asked Regan to help set it up and then invited all their friends. Caine sighed and pulled her closer, laying his hands on her rounded stomach. He wasn't usually so impulsive, but the thought of waiting to know if they were having a boy or girl for the days or weeks it would take Addison to plan a party to perfection made his skin twitch. Considering how unsure she'd looked when the ultrasound woman asked them if they wanted to know the gender, it was a safe bet she felt the same way.

So he'd called Regan and asked for a favor.

He just wished his stomach would unknot itself. The elevator doors opened and they walked down the hall to the door. *It's not too late to call the whole thing off and plan something out.* He took a deep breath, slipped the key into the lock, and let go of the crazy thought. It was too late to back out now. If Addison was angry, then he'd just have to find a way to make it up to her.

The only problem was how to make up the fact that he'd botched the gender reveal of their first child.

"Caine? Is everything okay?"

Shit. He made an effort to let go of the anxiety trying to take hold. "Yeah. The key's just stuck." He wiggled it a bit for emphasis and then there was nothing left to do but open the door and face the music.

They stepped into the condo and Addison gasped. "What's all this?"

The entire place was transformed. Paper banners hung from the archways in generic white and there were balloons everywhere. Regan and Brock stood on the other side of the living room, both grinning like fools, while the twins jumped on his white couch. Next to them was the entire crew from Connected at the Lips, and Addison's parents, practically radiating joy.

And his parents were here, too. They stood a little away from the group, but there was only a smile on his mother's face, and no sign of the tension that had plagued their relationship since he'd moved to New York.

Addison gaped at the group. "Mom? Dad? *James?*"

Her second-in-command grinned. "You didn't think we'd let you throw a party for the little tyke without us? He or she is going to be Connected at the Lips royalty."

Her mother smiled. "Honey, of course your father and I want to know if our first grandchild is a boy or girl." She shot a look at where Caine's nieces were still jumping on the couch. "Or, heaven forbid, twins."

Addison laughed, her hand going to her stomach. "Only one in here." She turned to him, her dark eyes shining. "You planned a surprise gender reveal party for me."

Was she upset? Angry? He couldn't tell. Caine took her hands. "If you don't want this, it's not too late—"

"I love it." She threw her arms around him and kissed him. "I love you."

One of the twins made a noise. "Gross."

"I love you, too."

Regan stepped out of Brock's arms with what looked suspiciously like a bounce. "Are you guys ready? James has agreed to be on picture duty, and the girls are helping, too."

One of them—Caine still had issues telling them apart—jumped from the couch to the floor. "Doggies!"

Regan grabbed her around the waist when she took off. "Yes, honey. Doggies." She looked at them. "Ready?"

Addison turned in his arms. "I'm ready."

Regan released her daughter and the pair raced down the hallway. A half a second later, they giggled and then a herd of dogs flew into the living room and Caine had to tighten his hold on Addison to keep her on her feet. "Down, boys!"

Then he saw what was attached to the back of their collars. Blue cloth. He reached down and pulled one free, and it unrolled into a tiny little shirt. "A boy?"

Addison already had two more blue shirts in her hand. "We're having a boy?"

Sheer joy nearly took Caine off his feet. A boy. He swept her into his arms and spun around, nearly tripping over the dogs. "A little boy." He met his father's gaze over her head. *I'm not going to make the same mistakes you did, but you're welcome to be a part of his life.* "A grandson."

His father nodded as if he received and understood the silent message, and a heaviness Caine hadn't even been aware of lifted from his shoulders. They were going to be all right. It might be a little bumpy with some growing pains, but it seemed like his parents wanted to make things right between them. He was only too happy to take that first step.

He went to his knees in front of her and rested his forehead on her stomach. "Hey, fella. I know you're going to be a little hell-raiser just like your Uncle Brock and I were, and I can't fucking wait."

Addison cleared her throat. "Maybe now's a good time to start working on language."

He laughed. "I can't *freaking* wait. I don't know if you're going to be a CEO like your daddy or a rocket scientist or something else entirely, but I'm going do my dam—*darnedest* to always be there to support you. I love you, little guy." He looked up. "And I love you."

She pressed a hand to her mouth. "This is...this is just perfect, Caine. Thank you."

"Not quite." He pushed to his feet and led her into the kitchen. Regan had come through here just like she had with everything else. He lifted the lid of the box in the middle of the counter, revealing the cake she'd been craving for the last few weeks.

"Okay, you're right. *Now* it's perfect."

Acknowledgments

To God, for constantly helping me find the light in all the shadows.

To Heather Howland, for helping me put all the pieces together and make this book the best it could be!

To Kari Olson, for loving Caine just as much as I do and for having an inspirational picture for every occasion to cheer me on!

To the Rabble, for being so freaking supportive and excited for each new book!

To my family, for being continually willing to let me meander through the worlds in my head and never complaining when dinner isn't quite perfectly put together.

To Tim, for being my shoulder to lean on always and the one person who can zen me out no matter how crazy the world around us gets.

And, finally, to Hawaii. Someday you'll get your happily ever after, and I can't wait!

About the Author

New York Times and USA TODAY bestselling author Katee Robert learned to tell stories at her grandpa's knee. She discovered romance novels and never looked back. When not writing sexy contemporary and speculative fiction romance novels, she spends her time playing imaginary games with her wee ones, driving her husband batty with what-if questions, and planning for the inevitable zombie apocalypse.

www.kateerobert.com

Find out where it began with Brock and Regan...

SEDUCING THE BRIDESMAID

a *Wedding Dare* novel by Katee Robert

Regan Wakefield is unafraid to go after what she wants, so she's thrilled when her friend's wedding offers her an opportunity to score Logan McCade, the practically perfect best man. Unfortunately, groomsman Brock McNeil keeps getting in her way, riling her up in the most delicious of ways. Regan may pretend the erotic electricity sparking between them is simply a distraction, but Brock will do whatever it takes to convince Regan that the best man for her is *him*.

Discover Katee Robert's NYT Bestselling **Come Undone** *series...*

WRONG BED, RIGHT GUY

CHASING MRS. RIGHT

TWO WRONGS, ONE RIGHT

SEDUCING MR. RIGHT

Introducing Katee's new **Out of Uniform** *series!*

IN BED WITH MR. WRONG

Air Force Pararescuer Ryan Flannery avoids his hometown at all costs, so he's not thrilled when he's set up on a blind date... until meets mousy librarian Brianne Nave. Her sweet curves and kissable lips are like a siren's call, but her smart mouth? Not so much. How can two people have so little chemistry outside the bedroom when they fit together so perfectly in it?

Stranded in a cabin by their friends, they'll be forced to find out—if they don't kill each other first.

HIS TO KEEP

Other books by Katee Robert

THE HIGH PRIESTESS

QUEEN OF SWORDS

QUEEN OF WANDS

CPSIA information can be obtained
at www.ICGtesting.com
Printed in the USA
BVHW03s1901020418
512272BV00001B/10/P